"Let's m... ...clear. There is not a damn thing I will do without you right now."

She stood very still. The sun had disappeared behind the hills, though there was enough light to still make her out. She wouldn't be able to see anything, even shapes in this light. Still, she moved unerringly into him, wrapping her arms around him.

A hug. A comfort.

He couldn't return it. He couldn't push her away. He could only stand there still as a statue, her arms around him and her cheek pressed to his chest.

"Hell, Rach. Be mad at me. Hate me. I can't stand you being nice to me right now."

"I guess it's too bad for you, because I can't stand to be mad at you right now." She pulled back, tilting her head up toward his. "If you told me right now, promised me right now, that you won't lie again, I'll believe you."

Even knowing he shouldn't, he placed his palm on her cheek. "I'm sorry. I can't do that."

BADLANDS BEWARE

NICOLE HELM

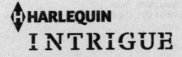

HARLEQUIN

INTRIGUE

For the family secrets that never get told.

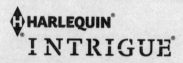

ISBN-13: 978-1-335-13660-2

Badlands Beware

Copyright © 2020 by Nicole Helm

Recycling programs
for this product may
not exist in your area.

This edition published by arrangement with Harlequin Books S.A.

For questions and comments about the quality of this book,
please contact us at CustomerService@Harlequin.com.

Harlequin Enterprises ULC
22 Adelaide St. West, 40th Floor
Toronto, Ontario M5H 4E3, Canada
www.Harlequin.com

Printed in U.S.A.

Nicole Helm grew up with her nose in a book and the dream of one day becoming a writer. Luckily, after a few failed career choices, she gets to follow that dream—writing down-to-earth contemporary romance and romantic suspense. From farmers to cowboys, Midwest to *the* West, Nicole writes stories about people finding themselves and finding love in the process. She lives in Missouri with her husband and two sons and dreams of someday owning a barn.

Books by Nicole Helm

Harlequin Intrigue

A Badlands Cops Novel

South Dakota Showdown
Covert Complication
Backcountry Escape
Isolated Threat
Badlands Beware

Carsons & Delaneys: Battle Tested

Wyoming Cowboy Marine
Wyoming Cowboy Sniper
Wyoming Cowboy Ranger
Wyoming Cowboy Bodyguard

Carsons & Delaneys

Wyoming Cowboy Justice
Wyoming Cowboy Protection
Wyoming Christmas Ransom

Stone Cold Texas Ranger
Stone Cold Undercover Agent
Stone Cold Christmas Ranger

Harlequin Superromance

A Farmers' Market Story

All I Have
All I Am
All I Want

Falling for the New Guy
Too Friendly to Date
Too Close to Resist

Visit the Author Profile page at Harlequin.com.

CAST OF CHARACTERS

Tucker Wyatt—A detective with the local county sheriff's department, Tucker is also working for the secretive North Star group trying to take down the Sons of the Badlands.

Rachel Knight—Duke Knight's only biological daughter, Rachel is an art teacher at the local reservation but handles most of the domestic work at the Knight Ranch. She was blinded and scarred at the age of three in a presumed animal attack.

Duke Knight—Rachel's father, who disappears in an effort to keep his daughters safe from his secret past.

Sarah Knight—Rachel's adopted sister, who works at the Knight Ranch.

Grandma Pauline Reaves—Tucker's grandmother who runs the neighboring ranch to the Knights.

Ace Wyatt—Tucker's father, former leader of the Sons of the Badlands, who is currently in jail.

Granger McMillan—Head of the North Star group.

Shay—North Star operative.

Jamison, Cody, Gage, Brady and Dev Wyatt—Tucker's brothers.

Chapter One

Rachel Knight had endured nightmares about the moment she'd lost the majority of her sight since she'd been that scared, injured three-year-old. The dream was always the same. The mountain lion. The surprising shock and pain of its attack.

Things she knew had happened, because what else could have attacked her? Because that was the truth that everyone believed. She'd somehow toddled out of the house and into the South Dakota ranchland only to have a run-in with a wild animal.

But in the dreams, there was always a voice. Not her father, or her late mother, or anyone who should have been there that night.

The voice of a stranger.

Rachel sucked in a breath as her eyes flew open. Her heart pounded, and her sheets were a sweaty tangle around her.

It was a dream. Nothing more and nothing less, but she couldn't figure out why twenty years after the attack she would still be so plagued by it.

Likely it was just all the danger that her family

had been facing lately. As much as she loved the Wyatts, both sturdy Grandma Pauline and her six law enforcement grandsons who owned the ranch next door, their connection to a vicious biker gang meant trouble seemed to follow wherever they went.

And somehow, this year it had also brought her foster sisters into the fold time and again. Putting them in jeopardy along with those Wyatt brothers— and then culminating in true love, against all odds.

All of their tormenters were in jail now, and Rachel wanted that to be the end of it.

But something about the dreams left her feeling edgy, like the next dangerous situation was just around the corner.

And that you'll get thrust into the path of one of the Wyatt boys and end up...

Rachel got out of bed without finishing the thought. Just because four of her five foster sisters had ended up in love with a Wyatt didn't mean she was doomed. Because if she was doomed, so was Sarah. Rachel laughed outright at the thought.

Sarah was too much like Pauline. Independent and prickly. The thought of her falling for *anyone*, let alone a bossy Wyatt, was unfathomable. Which meant it was inconceivable for Rachel, too. She might not be prickly, but she had no designs on ending up tied to a man with a dangerous past and likely even more dangerous secrets.

So, that was that.

Rachel went through her normal routine of showering and getting ready for the day before heading downstairs. She didn't have to tap her clock to hear the time to know it was earlier than she usually woke up.

She was—shudder—becoming a morning person. Maybe she could shed that with the coming winter.

It was full-on autumn now. Twenty-three was creeping closer and while she knew that wasn't old, she was exactly where she'd always been. Would she be stuck here forever? In the same house, on the same ranch, nothing ever changing except the people around her?

Teaching at the reservation offered some respite, but she was so dependent on others. If she moved somewhere with more public transportation, she could be independent.

And yet the thought of leaving South Dakota and her family always just made her sad. This was home. She wanted to be happy here, but there was a feeling of suffocation dogging her.

Maybe *that* was why she kept having those dreams.

Weirdly, that offered some comfort. There was a reason, and it was just feeling a little quarter-life crisis-y. Nothing…ominous.

She held on to that truth as she headed downstairs. Inside the house she never used her cane, even after the fire this summer. They'd fixed the affected sections to be exactly as they had been, which meant she knew it as well as she knew Pauline Reaves's ranch next door, or her classroom, or Cecilia's house on the rez where Rachel stayed when she was teaching.

She wasn't trapped. She had plenty of places to

go. As long as she didn't mind overprotective family everywhere she went.

Rachel stopped at the bottom of the stairs, surprised to hear someone in the kitchen. Duke's irritable mutterings alerted her to the fact it was her father before she could make out the shape of him.

Big, dark and the one constant presence in her life, aside from Sarah—who was the opposite of Duke. Small, petite and pale. She couldn't make out the details of a person's appearance, but she could recognize those she loved by the blurry shapes she could see out of her one eye that hadn't been completely blinded.

"Daddy, what are you doing?"

"What are you doing up?" he returned gruffly.

Rachel hesitated. While she often told her father everything that was going on with her, she tended to keep things that might worry him low-key. "I think my body finally got used to waking up early," she said, forcing a cheerfulness over it she didn't feel.

"Speaking of that…" He trailed off, approached her. His hand squeezed her shoulder. "Baby, I know you've got a class session coming up in a few weeks, but I think you should bow out. Too much has been going on."

Rachel opened her mouth, but no sound came out. Not teach at the rez? The art classes she held for a variety of age groups were short sessions and taught through the community rather than the school itself. She only instructed about twenty weeks out of the year, and he wanted her to miss a four-week session?

When teaching was the only thing that made her feel like she had a life outside of cooking and cleaning for Dad and Sarah.

"Just this session," Dad added. "Until we know for sure those Wyatt boys are done bringing their trouble around."

It felt like a slap in the face, but she didn't know how to articulate that. Except an unfair rage toward the Wyatts.

Rachel took a deep breath to calm herself. She never let her temper get the better of her. Mom had impressed upon her temper tantrums would never get her what she wanted. "I don't have anything to do with their trouble."

"I might have said the same about Felicity and Cecilia, but look what they endured this summer. It won't do."

"Dad, teaching those classes—"

"I know they mean a lot to you. And I am sorry. Maybe you could do some tutoring out here?"

"I'm an adult."

"You're twenty-two. I know this is a disappointment, but I'm not going to argue about it." His hand slid off her shoulder and she heard the jangle of keys.

Rachel frowned at how strange this all was. Maybe she was still dreaming. "Are you *going* somewhere?"

There was a pregnant pause. "Just into town on some errands."

Her frown deepened. Sarah took care of almost all the errands now that it was just the two of them left living with Duke. Her father almost never ventured into town. And he never gave *her* unreasonable ultimatums.

"What's wrong, Dad?" she asked gravely.

"I want my girls safe," he said, and she heard his retreating footsteps as though that was that.

She fisted her hands on her hips. Oh, no, it was *not*. And she was going to get some answers. If they wouldn't come from her father, they'd just have to come from the source of the trouble.

TUCKER WYATT HAD always loved spending nights at his grandmother's house. Though he kept an apartment in town, he'd much rather spend time with his family at the Reaves ranch.

Until now.

He sighed. Why had he ever thought his current predicament was a good idea? He was *terrible* at keeping secrets.

Case in point, he was about 75 percent sure his brother Brady had figured out that Tucker *accidentally* stumbling into a situation where he could help save Brady's life from one of their father's protégés wasn't so accidental. That it was part of his working beyond his normal job as detective with the Valiant County Sheriff's Department.

And, since their youngest brother had been kicked out of North Star Group just a few months ago, it didn't take a rocket scientist to figure out what group Tucker might also be working for.

He was going to have to quit. The North Star

Group had approached him because of his ties to Ace Wyatt, former head of the dangerous Sons of the Badlands, and a few of Tucker's cases that involved other high-ranking officials in the Sons.

Cases Tuck had been sure were private and confidential. But those words didn't mean much to North Star.

They'd wanted him on the Elijah Jones investigation, but then Brady and Cecilia Mills, one of the Knight girls, had gotten in the way.

The only reason Tucker hadn't been kicked out of North Star, as far as he could see, was because the North Star higher-ups didn't know his brother and Cecilia were suspicious of Tucker's involvement.

Which didn't sit right. Surely they didn't think his brother, a police officer, didn't have questions about a mysterious explosion that took Elijah Jones down enough to be restrained, hospitalized and, as of today, transferred to prison.

It had been a mess of a summer all in all, but things would assuredly calm down now. Ace was in maximum-security prison and Elijah was going to jail, along with a variety of his helpers.

But as long as Tucker was part of North Star and their continued efforts to completely and utterly destroy the Sons of the Badlands, he wouldn't feel totally settled *or* calm.

The back door that came into the kitchen swung open—not all that unusual. Grandma Pauline always had people coming and going through this entrance, but Tuck was surprised by the appearance of a *very* angry looking Rachel Knight.

She pointed directly at him, as if he'd done something wrong. "What's going on with my dad?"

Tuck stared at Rachel in confusion. She looked... pissed, which was not her norm. She was probably the most even-keeled of the whole Knight bunch.

While her sisters had all been fostered or adopted by Duke and Eva Knight, Rachel was their lone biological daughter. She didn't look much like her father—more favored her late mother, which always gave Tuck a bit of a pang.

His memories of his own mother weren't pleasant. He'd had Grandma Pauline, who he loved with his whole heart. Her influence on him and his brothers when they'd come to live with her meant the world to him.

But Eva Knight had been a soft, motherly presence in the Reaves-Knight world. Even if she'd been next door and not their mother, she'd treated them like sons. He'd never seen anything that matched it.

Except in her daughter. Tall and slender, Rachel had Eva's sharp nose and high cheekbones and long black hair. The biggest difference were the scars around Rachel's eyes, lines of lighter brown against the darker skin color on the rest of her face.

She could *see*, but not clearly. It always seemed to Tuck that her dark brown eyes were a little too knowing.

At least on *this* he wasn't keeping a secret—and

failing at it. He had no idea why she'd demand of him anything about Duke Knight.

"Well?" she demanded as he only sat there like a deer caught in headlights.

"I haven't the slightest idea what's going on with your father. Why would I?"

"I don't know. I only know it has something do with *you*."

By the way she flung her arms in the air, he could only assume she didn't mean him personally but the whole of the Wyatts.

"Why don't we sit down?" He took her elbow gently to lead her to the table. "Back up. Talk about this, you know, calmly."

She tugged her elbow out of his grasp, clearly not wanting to sit. "He doesn't want me teaching this fall. He's worried about our safety. I know it doesn't have to do with *my* family. So, it has to do with yours."

Tucker held himself very still—an old trick he had down to an art these days. Letting his temper get the best of him as a kid had gotten the crap beaten out of him. Routinely.

Ace had told him his emotions would be the death of him if he didn't learn to control them. Hone them.

Tucker refused to *hone* them or be anything like his father. Which meant also never letting his temper boil over. He pictured a blue sky, puffy white clouds and a hawk arcing through both.

When he trusted his voice, he spoke and offered a smile. "I guess that's possible." He didn't allow himself to say what he wanted to. *Your sisters seem to be*

getting my brothers in trouble plenty on their own.
"I'm not sure specifically what it could be that would
have Duke worried about you teaching at the rez. Did
something happen? Maybe Cecilia would know."

"What would I know?" Cecilia asked, walking
into the kitchen. She was in her tribal police uniform, likely on her way to work. Though she was
still nursing some wounds from her run in with
Ace's protege and hadn't been cleared for active
duty, she'd started in-house hours this week.

Though Duke and Eva Knight had fostered Cecilia, like Rachel she was a blood relation—Eva's
niece. But she had been raised as "one of the Knight
girls" as much Rachel's sister as her cousin.

"Has there been any new trouble at the rez that
might make Duke nervous about Rach teaching her
upcoming session?" Tucker asked.

Rachel scowled at him. "I wasn't going to bring
her into it, jerk."

Cecilia's brow puckered. "I haven't heard anything. Dad doesn't want you teaching? Kind of late
to have concerns about that, isn't it? Doesn't your
session start the first of the month? And why didn't
you want to bring me into it?"

Rachel sighed heavily. "Yes, it does, and yes, it's
late." She looked pointedly in Tucker's direction, but
when she spoke it was to Cecilia. "I wasn't going to
bring you into it, because obviously it's not about
you. I don't think it's about the rez, either. I think
it's about the Wyatts."

"Look, Rach, I know the Wyatts are an easy target, no offense, Tuck. But if something bad was going on over here, Brady would have told me."

Because Cecilia and Brady now shared a *room* at his grandmother's house, a simple fact Tucker wasn't used to. Four of his brothers all paired off. And with the Knight girls of all people. It was sudden and weird.

But he just had to keep that to himself. Especially when Brady and Cecilia lived here now. "Well, I'll let you ladies figure this out. I've got a meeting to get to," Tucker said, quickly slipping past Rachel even as she began to protest.

Whatever was going on with Duke and Rachel was not his business, and he had to meet with his boss at North Star to nip this whole mission in the bud. It wasn't for him. He was a detective, and a damn good one, but he would never become adept at lying to his family.

He got in his truck, and drove to the agreed upon location. A small diner in Rapid City. Tucker had never met Granger McMillan, the head of the North Star Group. He'd been approached by field operatives and dealt with them solely.

Until now.

Tucker scanned the diner. Granger had said he'd know who he was, and Tucker had thought that was a little over-the-top cloak-and-dagger, but the large man in a cowboy hat and dark angry eyes sitting in the corner was *quite* familiar.

The man he was sitting across from turned in his seat, looked right at Tucker and gestured him over.

Tucker moved forward feeling a bit like he'd taken a blow to the head. Why was Duke here? What *was* this?

"You two know each other," the man, who could only be Granger McMillan, said. Not a question. A statement. "Have a seat, Wyatt. We have a lot to discuss."

Chapter Two

Rachel didn't get anywhere with Cecilia. Falling in love had certainly colored her vision when it came to the Wyatts. It was a disappointment, but one that was hard to hold on to when Brady had come in and he'd exchanged a casual goodbye kiss with her sister.

She would have never put Brady and Cecilia together, but when they were together, it seemed so *right*. Two pieces clicking together to mellow each other out a bit.

But even if that softened her up, Rachel wasn't ready to give up on being mad at the Wyatt brothers. So, she sought out someone she knew would back her up.

Sarah wiped her brow with the back of her arm. She'd been hefting water buckets into the truck to move them to a different pasture while Rachel laid out her case.

"Yeah, it's weird Dad took off, but what do you want me to do about it? I'm kind of running a ranch single-handedly here while he's doing whatever." Dev Wyatt's dogs raced around Sarah and Rachel.

"My biggest concern is why I suddenly have two dogs. I did not consent to these dogs."

Rachel patted Cash on the head. Sarah talked a big game, but Rachel had overheard her just last night loving on the very dogs she was currently irritated over.

With a pang, Rachel missed Minnie, her old service dog. She knew she should start working on getting another one, or maybe even work on training her own, but it just made her sad still.

"What do you need help with?" Rachel asked, feeling guilty about unloading on her sister when she was so busy. The Knight ranch wasn't the biggest operation in South Dakota, but Duke and Sarah had to work really hard to make it profitable, and with all the danger around lately, hiring outside help felt like too big a risk.

"It's fine," Sarah replied, hopping off the truck bed and closing the gate. "Dev's coming over this afternoon to help. Maybe he'll take those stupid mutts back with him."

Even if Sarah could convince the dogs to go back with Dev, Rachel knew Sarah was all talk. She'd be bribing the dogs back over by suppertime.

"Well, I'll go make up some sandwiches for lunch. Want some pasta salad to go with it?"

"Yes, please."

Rachel walked back to the house over the well-worn path along the fence that led her to and from the stables. She moved through her normal chore of preparing lunch for Sarah and Dad, though Dad still wasn't home.

Rachel set the water to boil for pasta salad and frowned. It wasn't like her father to run errands on a ranch morning, even more unlike him to be gone for hours at a time. Cecilia had seemed concerned, but not enough to miss work. Plus, now she was going to tell Brady and he'd talk about it with his brothers and Rachel was fed up with Wyatts interfering.

Ughhh, those Wyatts. Rachel let herself bang around in the kitchen. She supposed Cecilia was a *little* right and Rachel was *maybe* projecting some feelings on them because it was safer than being upset with her father.

But Rachel didn't really care about being fair or balanced in the privacy of her own thoughts. Pasta salad and sandwiches made, she set them in the fridge and went to handling the rest of her normal chores, grumbling to herself the whole way.

Duke and Sarah were terrible housekeepers, so Rachel was often the default cleaner in the house. She didn't mind it, though. Having things to do made her feel useful. She tidied, swept, vacuumed, even dusted. She went upstairs and made the beds. Once she was done, she tapped her clock for the time.

The robotic voice told her it was nearly noon. Still no Sarah and even worse, no Dad. Rachel headed downstairs, wracking her brain for some reason her father would be gone this long without telling her.

She stopped halfway down the stairs. A horrible thought dawned on her. What if he was sick? Like

Mom. What if he was at the doctor getting terrible news he wanted to hide?

The thought had tears stinging her eyes. She couldn't do it. She couldn't lose her mom and her dad before she was even twenty-five. Before she found a significant other. Before she had kids. Dad had to be around for that. Mom couldn't, so Dad *had* to be.

Rachel marched toward his room, propelled by fear masked as fury. If something was wrong, she'd find evidence of it there.

She stepped inside. He'd moved down to the main floor with Mom when she had gotten sick. He'd never moved back upstairs. Sometimes Rachel worried about him wallowing in the loss. Now she worried the same fate was waiting for him.

No. I refuse.

She tidied up, deciding it was an easy excuse to poke around his things. Which wasn't out of the norm. When she deep-cleaned the house, she took care of Dad's room. She didn't find anything out of the ordinary, though she wouldn't be able to read any of the medicine bottles to tell if there was something off there—but based on the number and size there didn't seem to be anything more than the usual over-the-counter painkiller and heartburn medicines.

She'd need Sarah to read the labels to be sure, but then she'd have to bring her sister into this and Sarah had enough to worry about with the ranch.

She pondered the dilemma as she made Dad's bed. As she adjusted the pillows, she felt something cool and hard. She reached out and touched her fingers to the object. It was a black blob in her vision, but she quickly realized she was touching a gun.

Rachel stood frozen in place for a good minute, pillow held up in one hand, her other hand grasping the gun. It wasn't that her father didn't have firearms. He had a few hunting rifles, kept in the safe in the basement. He had one hung above the back door because after reading the *Little House* books to her, he'd decided that's where one needed to go.

But this was a small pistol. Like the ones the Wyatt boys carried when on duty. And it was under his pillow. Carefully she picked it up and felt around some more, getting an idea of the gun model before she checked the chamber.

Loaded, which seemed very unsafe in his *bed*. Rachel didn't know what to make of it, but his whole talk about safety sure made it seem like he was worried about some kind of threat.

What on earth kind of threat would Duke be facing?

"Rachel?"

She nearly dropped the gun at Sarah's voice. Luckily, it came from the kitchen, not from right next to her. She quickly slipped the gun back under the pillow, left the bed unmade and tiptoed into the hallway.

"Coming!" she called, trying to steady her beating heart. Sarah didn't need to know about this. Not just yet. First, Rachel had to figure what was going on.

"So, what you're telling me…" Tucker raked his fingers through his hair, not knowing whether to look at Duke or Granger "…is Knight ranch was a witness protection hideout."

Duke's gaze was patently unfriendly, which was odd coming from a man he'd always looked up to. Tucker had grown up in a biker gang surrounded by nothing but bad. Ever since he'd gotten out, Duke had been there. Grandma Pauline and Eva had been mother figures. Duke had been the father figure.

But Duke clearly didn't want Granger letting Tucker in on his past. His *true* identity. How did Duke Knight of all people have a *true* identity?

"And the girls don't know?"

"Why would they know?" Duke asked, his voice a raspy growl. "I left that old life behind over thirty-five years ago. Met Eva two years later, and we built this family on who I was *now*, not who I was *then*. Then was gone, and has been for a very long time."

"A cop." Duke Knight had been a cop. A cop who, in his first year on duty, had taken down a powerful family of dirty police officers. And then had a bounty put on his head and had to be moved into WITSEC.

A ranch in the middle of nowhere South Dakota sure made sense, and feeling safe enough to find a wife and build a family here made even more sense. But Tucker didn't know how to accept it.

"Grandma Pauline… She had to know."

Duke shrugged. "Don't know if she did or didn't, but Pauline never asked any questions. Never poked her nose into my business." He looked pointedly at Granger.

Granger, who was here for a current reason. That somehow involved Tucker. "Why would this group want to come after you when thirty-five years have passed? Wouldn't it be water under the bridge?"

"You're Ace Wyatt's son and you really have to ask that question?"

Tuck was chastened enough at that. When fear was currency, the years didn't matter so much. Only proving your strength, your ability to destroy did.

Tucker turned to face Granger across from him at the diner table. "And how does this connect to North Star?"

"We've been working under the assumption Vince MacLean was casing your grandmother's ranch because of the Wyatt connection, which is why we brought you in," Granger said. Facts Tucker was well aware of.

Granger was a tall man, dressed casually. A layperson might not think anything of someone like him, sitting in a diner, having a friendly cup of coffee. But Tucker saw all the signs of someone on alert. The way his gaze swept the establishment. The way he filed away everyone who entered or exited.

"We couldn't quite figure his role out. But the information you've passed along to us, plus what we already had, started to point to the fact there might be a different target." Granger nodded toward Duke. "We started looking into not just who Vince was directly reporting to, but who the people he was reporting to passed information to and so on. What we found is a connection to the Vianni family."

Tucker didn't need to be led to the rest. "Who were the family of dirty cops you took down?"

Duke nodded.

"We started digging into the family, into possible connections, and figured out Duke's. Since he was the target, we brought him in. And now we're bringing you in. The Sons connecting to the Vianni family is an expansion. It gives both groups more reach, and makes them stronger than they were."

"The Sons have been weakened."

"You can keep throwing their leaders in jail, Wyatt, but that doesn't end their infrastructure or ability to regroup."

"What does?" Tucker returned.

Granger's gaze, which had been cool and controlled up to this point, heated with fury. But his voice remained calm as he spoke. "We need Duke to help us. Which means he has to disappear for a little while. Duke's not too keen on leaving his ranch or his daughters."

"Nor should he be," Tucker snapped, his own temper straining. "Have you been paying attention these past few months? Duke being gone doesn't make the threat go away." He turned to Duke, who was sitting next to him in the booth. "You're leaving them to be a new target, that's all. And you—" Tucker faced Granger "—you're caring about your own North Star plots and plans without thinking about innocent lives."

Tucker didn't wilt when Granger lifted his eyebrows regally. "Watch your step, boy. I know more about protecting innocent lives than you could even begin to imagine. But Duke is our key between the Sons and the Viannis, and without him, more innocent people get hurt. A lot more."

Tucker whipped his gaze back to Duke, too angry to be chastened by Granger's words. "You didn't tell any of us? This whole time you knew you were a target and you didn't think to give us a heads-up so we could help?"

"I didn't want to bring you or your brothers into it. I don't want my daughters brought into it, and that's all your brothers seem capable of doing." Duke nodded toward Granger. "His father is the reason I have the ranch I do. The life I do. When Granger here came to me… I might not like it, but I owe the McMillan family, and I owe it to the other people the Viannis have hurt after I bowed out."

Tucker snorted in derision. Maybe he should have felt sorry for Duke, but all he could think about was Rachel already coming to him worried about her father. "You think your girls are going to buy you *leaving*?"

"It'll be your job to convince them," Granger said matter-of-factly, like that was a mission anyone could accomplish. He pushed a manila envelope over to Tucker. "This includes a letter to the daughters from Duke, a packet of fake vacation itinerary. You'll take it to Sarah and Rachel and say you found it—where and how is up to you." Then Granger slid a phone across the table. "You'll also take this. It's been programmed with your cell number, as well as a se-

cret number that will allow contact with someone at
North Star directly. We'll reach you through this if
we need you. It's also got access to security measures
set up around the Reaves and Knight ranches, thanks
to your brother. He has no idea you have access to
any of this, and no one in your family or Duke's can
know, either. Is that understood?"

Tucker looked at the folder and the phone. None
of this made sense, and how on earth was he going
to convince Sarah and Rachel—and the rest of either family for that matter—that Duke, who'd barely
left the ranch even for errands throughout all their
lives, was going on vacation. Suddenly, and without
warning. "You can't be serious."

"Oh, I'm deadly serious, Wyatt. And so is this."

Chapter Three

"Something has to be wrong." Rachel stood in Grandma Pauline's kitchen, Sarah next to her. She could hear the dogs whining outside, but Grandma Pauline did not allow dogs in her kitchen.

"If he'd come home before dinner, I wouldn't think *too* much of it. But he still isn't back and he won't answer his cell," Sarah said, wringing her hands together.

"I called Gage," Brady offered. "He's going to head over to Valiant County and see if he can sweet talk them into putting some men on it before the required hours for a missing person. Then he'll look himself. Cecilia said she's going to ask around town after her shift, too. If he's around, one of them will find him."

"What do you mean *if*?" Sarah demanded. "Where else would he go?"

Which echoed the fear growing inside of Rachel. "Do you think something happened to him?" she asked, straight out. Because if Brady Wyatt thought something had happened to him, his instincts were most likely right.

Brady's response was grim. "Duke left the ranch of his own volition, but you were concerned about him being worried about danger. Maybe there's something he wasn't telling us."

The door opened and Tucker entered. Aside from Brady and Gage, Rachel could tell the difference in the Wyatt brothers by general shape. Even though they were all tall and broad, they had a different presence about them.

If she took a lot of time, she could figure out Gage and Brady, but being twins made it a bit more difficult, and she could always tell from their voices.

But Tucker was always a slightly…lighter presence. His hair wasn't so dark, his movements were always a little easier. But something about the way he entered the kitchen now was all wrong.

"Hey, all. What's going on?"

Rachel frowned. He did *not* sound his usual cheerful self. Something was weighing on him, and that was clear as day in his voice.

"Duke's missing," Sarah said plainly.

"Missing?"

"We can't find him. He hasn't come back to the ranch since this morning."

"You're sure he's not out in the fields?" Tucker asked.

"No. I'm worrying everyone because I didn't look around the ranch," Sarah replied sarcastically. "Don't be an ass, Tuck."

"I'm sure there's a rational explanation. If you're all worried, I can—"

"We've already got Gage and Cecilia on it," Brady said.

There was something off about Tucker. Something…odd in the way he delivered his responses.

"Oh, I picked up your mail," he offered as if it he'd just remembered. "It was falling out of the box."

Rachel assumed he put it into Sarah's hands before he moved over to the table. "I didn't have a chance to get dinner. You got any leftovers, Grandma?" He moved farther into the kitchen, still acting…strangely. But no one else seemed to notice, so maybe she was taking her worry about Dad and spreading it around.

There was a thud and the flutter of papers. "There's a letter from Dad," Sarah screeched. The sound of the envelope being ripped open had Rachel moving closer even though she wouldn't be able to read it.

Sarah read aloud. "Dear girls, I know you probably won't be able to believe this, but I've decided it's time for a break. If I don't go right now, I know I never will. I've included my vacation itinerary so you don't worry, but this is something I need to do for myself. Take good care of each other. Love, Dad."

"There's no possible way," Rachel croaked, panic hammering at her throat. "Maybe he wrote that, but not because he wanted to take a vacation. Not of his own volition." Nothing would drag her father away from the ranch, away from his daughters. Not even temporarily.

"And he'd never leave without someone here to help me," Sarah added, her voice uncharacteristically tremulous. "I can't handle the ranch on my own."

"We'll work it out," Dev said gruffly. "Don't worry about the ranch. Brady—"

"We'll tell Gage the latest development," Brady said before Dev could instruct him. "He can—"

"Let me look into it," Tucker said. "I'm the detective. We don't need to get Valiant County involved or have Gage and Cecilia asking around."

"We can *all* look into it," Brady said evenly.

"Yeah, but if we all start looking into it, and something *is* wrong, we've alerted everyone we know. But if I look into it, pretend like I'm just researching one of my cases, we might be able to unearth whatever trouble there actually is without causing suspicion. *If* there's any trouble at all."

"My father did not go on a *vacation.* Period. Let alone without telling us. What kind of trouble would he be in?"

"I don't know, Rach. Let me look into it. If there's trouble, we'll find it."

"Yes, you're very good at finding it," she replied caustically.

"Now, now," Grandma Pauline said, and though the words might have been gentle coming from most grandmothers, from Pauline it was a clear warning.

Rachel blew out a breath.

Tucker's voice was very calm when he spoke, and

she could easily imagine him using that tone with a hysterical person on a call. He would promise to take care of everything no matter how upset the person was.

She swallowed at the lump of fear and anxiety in her throat. Tucker could do that because he wanted to help people. She wanted to blame him for all the trouble right now, but deep down she knew it wasn't his fault or his brothers' faults.

The Wyatts were good men who wanted to do the right thing, and she had to stop sniping at them. Division was not going to bring her father home.

"What can we do? While you're looking for him?" she asked of Tuck. "We can't just sit around waiting."

"Unfortunately, I think you *should* sit and wait. If there's danger, and we're not sure there is, we want to know what kind before we go wading in. What we do know is that even if he is in danger, he's alive. He left of his own accord. He's made *some* kind of decision here."

"He could have been threatened to leave," Sarah pointed out. "Blackmailed. Though over what I don't have a clue."

"Yes," Tucker agreed equitably. "If that's the case, someone wanted him to leave of his own accord. Think how easy it would be to ambush a man like Duke. How often he's out in the fields or barn or stables alone. This is more than Duke being in life-threatening danger. It's deeper and more complicated. *If* it's anything other than a mid-life crisis."

Rachel scoffed simultaneously with Sarah.

"He's not wrong," Grandma Pauline said. "Duke hasn't been himself lately. Wouldn't be unheard of for someone in their late fifties to have a bit of a personal crisis."

Rachel felt like the world had been upended. Why were her and Sarah the only ones freaking out about this? How could Grandma Pauline stand there and say her father was having a *personal crisis*?

"I'll head back into the office right now. Get the ball rolling on an investigation. I'll update you all in the morning."

No one spoke, not to argue with Tucker or demand more answers. Rachel had to believe they were in as much shock as she was. This couldn't actually be happening.

And Tucker wasn't acting right. She couldn't put her finger on what was wrong, just that something *was*. She heard him exit, the normal conversation picking back up. Sarah and Dev discussing ranch concerns, Brady on the phone with Jamison, the oldest Wyatt brother, giving him an update, and Grandma Pauline fussing around the kitchen cleaning up.

Didn't any of them feel it? Didn't any of them… She shook her head and slipped out the kitchen door. She couldn't make out Tucker's shape in the low light of dusk, but she didn't hear a car engine so he hadn't made it that far yet.

She took a few steps forward until she could make out the shape of him. "What aren't you telling us?"

She could tell he turned to face her, but she didn't

have the ability to read his expression. Still there was a lot in that long careful pause.

"If there was anything I could tell you to make sense of this, I would."

She wasn't sure why that made her want to cry instead of yell at him. Which left her unsure of what to say.

He stepped close, then his hands were giving hers a squeeze. "I'm going to do everything I can to bring him home safe, Rach. Whether he's in trouble or not. You believe that, don't you?"

She wasn't sure what she believed in the midst of all this insanity, but in her heart she knew Tucker was a good man and that he loved her father. Maybe none of this made sense, but he wouldn't promise to do everything he could and then not.

"Yeah, I do."

He gave her hands one last squeeze, released them. "Good. I'll have an update in the morning. I promise." Then he left her standing in the cool evening, unsure of how to work through all her emotions, and all her fears.

It was a lot of work. Not looking for Duke, and trying to undo all his brothers had already set in motion. Tucker couldn't very well have the entire Valiant County Sheriff's Department out searching for Duke. Even if North Star hid Duke or used him for whatever their plan was, having people sniffing around just wasn't going to be good.

Tucker scrubbed his hands over his face. Granger

hadn't given him much to go on. Just that he had to make sure the Knights thought Duke was on vacation while they did the hard work.

When North Star had first approached Tucker, it had been through a lower operative. The woman had told him they had reason to believe Vince MacLean was gathering intel on the Wyatts, and to do whatever he could to find out who Vince was reporting to.

It had been a simple mission, straightforward and in Tuck's own best interest to help his family. And it had, in fact, helped his family a great deal as his following Vince had led him straight to Brady and Cecilia when they were in trouble.

Tucker locked up his office and headed for his car. He'd have liked to head back to the ranch, but it was two in the morning and he needed to catch a few hours of sleep.

He didn't know how he was going to face Rachel. He hadn't lied to her. He *would* do everything he could to bring Duke safely home. Tucker just didn't know how much of a say he had in things. But the one thing he *did* know? That he was never going to convince her Duke had taken a vacation of his own accord.

He headed for his car. The night was dark, the station mostly deserted. Still, the feeling of being watched had him slowly, carefully resting his hand on the butt of his weapon strapped to his belt.

"No need, Wyatt."

He didn't recognize the female's voice, but when she materialized out of the dark, he recognized her as the woman who'd originally contacted him about North Star.

"What now?" he muttered. Instead of stopping, he kept moving for his car. He wasn't too keen on being accommodating to the North Star crew right now, considering they were making his life unduly complicated. He kept one hand on his gun for good measure.

"There's chatter. Some people know Duke's missing."

"Yeah. Like his entire family? They're worried about him, because no one in their right mind is going to believe Duke Knight left South Dakota to go on *vacation*."

"Like the Sons. From what I've been able to gather, they think the Viannis got him. While they think that, there are certain parties who are going to be interested in friends of the Wyatts being unprotected, so to speak."

Tuck tossed his bag in the passenger side of his car. He was tired and irritable and this wasn't helping. "And who's fault would that be?"

"Look, I'm trying to be friendly here. I know enough about the setup from your brother. Someone needs to keep an eye on the Knight ranch. Just because the Viannis are focused on Duke, doesn't mean the Sons won't focus on a weakness in the Wyatts' armor if they can find one. Last I heard, the Knights are a weakness."

"I'm pretty sure I told your boss to be just as worried about Duke Knight's daughters as he was about Duke. He didn't seem too concerned."

"Yeah, because his concern is the mission."

"And what's your concern?"

She muttered something incomprehensible under her breath. "Watch their backs, huh?"

"Why don't you go talk to my brother about it?"

"Because your brother got kicked out, pal. You, on the other hand, are in the thick of things. So, grow a pair." She melted back into the dark shadows before he could retort.

Which was for the best. No use taking his nasty mood out on someone who was trying to help.

Especially when she was right. Sarah and Rachel alone in the Knight house, even with Dev's dogs, just wasn't a good idea. He wouldn't be surprised to hear that Cecilia had decided to spend the night over there herself, and she was trained law enforcement.

She'd also been injured not that long ago, and Brady still wasn't on active duty due to his injuries. They'd saved an innocent child from being taken into the Sons, but they hadn't come out unscathed.

So, sending him over there to spend the night with Cecilia wasn't enough of a comfort. Dev would be helping out with ranching duties, but he'd been a cop for all of six months before he'd sustained serious injuries that left him with a limp.

Thanks to dear old Dad.

Jamison and Cody both lived in Bonesteel, and while he knew they'd all pitch in to help, it'd bring Cody's young daughter and Jamison's even younger sister-in-law into the fray and they deserved to be as far from danger as possible after what they'd endured when Ace Wyatt had come after them and their families. The only other option was Gage and Felicity, who both worked almost two hours away. Not to mention, Felicity was pregnant.

Which left him. He didn't mind that. He was happy to protect whomever needed protecting. It was the convincing the women involved they *needed* protecting that was going to be the headache. On top of the one he already had.

Tucker slid into his car. There was no going to his apartment now. Even if it was the middle of the night, he needed to head to the ranches. He had to figure out a way to convince Rachel and Sarah it was best if he stayed with them for a while.

As he drove through the thick of night, he considered just telling everyone the truth. What could the North Star Group do to him? He didn't owe them silence. And with the whole Wyatt clan in on things, wasn't it possible they could help take down the Viannis and the Sons themselves?

The list of reasons not to have his brothers spend the night at the Knight house went through his head. Because for all the same reasons, it didn't feel right to bring them into this. They'd built new lives, survived their own near-death injuries. And what had he done? All this time, all these months of danger and threats from Ace and the Sons, and he'd *investigated*. Between his brothers and their significant others, they'd all been tortured, shot, temporarily blinded and more.

Tucker had fought off a few Sons goons, but had mostly emerged unscathed.

So, no, he couldn't tell them. It was his turn to take on the danger, take on the Sons. His turn to protect his family, and the Knight girls.

Whether they wanted protecting or not.

Chapter Four

Rachel woke up from the nightmare in a cold sweat. The recurrence so soon after the last one made sense. She was stressed and worried. Of course, she'd have terrible dreams to go along with those terrible feelings.

But there'd been no mountain lion in this nightmare. She sat up and rubbed her eyes and then hugged herself against the chill.

The mountain lion had been a man. She could still visualize him. Blue eyes glowing, burn scars all over the side of one face. She could hear his voice in her head, rough and growly with an odd regional American accent she couldn't place.

She shuddered. It was a *dream*. Yeah, a creepy one that was still lodged in her head, but it was fiction. Dreams weren't real.

Though this one had felt particularly, scarily real.

She got out of bed even though it was still dark. She didn't bother to check the time. Too early. She'd just go downstairs and get a drink of water. Hopefully, it would help settle her.

She was safe. Maybe Dad wasn't, but she was. Here in this house, with Cecilia and Sarah down the hall. Though she felt a little guilty that Cecilia had insisted on spending the night since Brady had to stay at Grandma Pauline's due to his leg injury.

She wished she could say her and Sarah could handle it, but while they could manage anything around the ranch, they weren't trained law enforcement, and they didn't have any background or experience in fighting off bad guys.

Cecilia did. In fact, *everyone* else did. Rachel blew out a breath as she tiptoed downstairs. She stopped at the bottom, frowning at the odd sound. Like the scrape of a chair against the floor.

Her breath caught, pulse going wild as panic filled her. Someone was in the kitchen. Someone was—

"What are you doing up?"

Tucker's voice. Coming from the kitchen table. The *Knight* kitchen table. Long before sunrise.

"What are you doing here? It's…dark still."

"Honestly? I got a little tip that I shouldn't be letting you two be here alone. A friendly tip, but still. I thought it was better if I headed over here rather than stayed the night in my apartment."

"You didn't need to do that. Cecilia's here. We have our law enforcement contingent."

"Good." But he made no excuses to leave. Instead, they stood there, together in the dark.

"Which means you don't have to stay," she continued. She wasn't sure why she'd said that. It was a nice thing he was doing, and she should be thanking him. But she was braless in her pajamas and Tucker Wyatt was in her kitchen. She crossed her arms over her chest.

"Unfortunately, I don't agree."

She scowled in his general direction, whether he could see it or not. "A penis is not the protector of womankind, Tucker."

He sighed heavily. "I never said it was, but Cecilia is still recovering from her injuries. It's good she's here. She'll be able to notice and address a threat, but will she be able to neutralize it? No one heard me pick the lock, did they?"

"You picked the lock?" she screeched.

He immediately shushed her, which did not do anything to make her feel better about the situation. "It's just a precaution. Regardless of what's going on with Duke, the Sons know he's missing. We don't want them looking at you as easy pickings."

"Because I'm blind," she said flatly.

"Because we don't know where this threat is coming from, if it's coming. I don't think Sarah should be out in the fields alone, and I don't think you should be in this house alone. And before you lecture me about sexism, it isn't about your gender, it's about numbers. When there's danger, two is better than one."

"Then I can accompany Sarah out in the fields, and *you* aren't needed."

"What do you have against me, Rach?" His voice was soft. Not sad exactly, but there was a thread of... hurt in his voice. "I thought we were friends, but you seem to have something very specifically against *me* right now."

"I don't."

"You're sure acting like you do."

"I…" She felt like an absolute jerk, which wasn't fair. She wasn't acting like she had anything against Tucker. He was just…

She felt him approach and his hands rested on her shoulders. "I know it's a tough time. I'm not trying to make it tougher. I'm honestly just trying to help. Can you let me do that?"

There was no way to say no and maintain that she was a reasonable human being, which she *was*. Plus, he was giving her shoulders a squeeze—a kind, reassuring gesture. He smelled like stale coffee and she wondered if he'd been up all night worrying over Duke and his girls.

It made her heart pinch. Here he was, doing all he could to find out what was going on with her father, and she was taking out her fear and anxiety on him. She sighed. "Of course I can," she said gently. "I'm not trying to be difficult. I'm just scared."

He gave her a light peck on the temple. It was something he'd always done. Tuck was the sweet Wyatt brother, if you could call any of them sweet. He had an easy affectionate streak, and he often comforted with a hug or a casual, friendly kiss.

But his hands lingered, even if his lips didn't. Rachel didn't know why she noticed…why she felt something odd skitter along her skin.

Then he cleared his throat, his hands dropping as

he stepped away, and she didn't have to think about it any longer.

"I think it'd be best if I stay here," he reiterated. His voice had an odd note to it that disappeared as he continued to speak. "It'll help my investigation, and after the fire, we can't be too careful about threats that can get through Cody's safety measures. Everything I've found points to Duke leaving of his own accord."

Before Rachel could object to that, Tucker rolled right on.

"I'm not saying he left because he wanted to. I'm just saying he did it on his own two feet. No one dragged him away. Even if he didn't take a vacation like he's saying, there might be a reason. One that doesn't mean he's in immediate danger. It could be he's trying to protect you girls."

"You don't really think that."

"Actually, so far? It's exactly what I think. You don't have to agree with me, Rach. You just have to give me some space to stay here and keep an eye on things, and maybe go through Duke's room."

"And if I say no?"

"Well, I'll go through the rest of your sisters until someone agrees."

She huffed out an irritated breath. Of course he would, and one of her sisters would. But he could have barged in there and done it without any permission, so she would have to give him points for that. "I guess you could stay in his room, and if you poke around, it wouldn't be any of my business."

"Great," he said, sounding a mixture of pleased and relieved. "Hey, you should go back to bed. It's three in the morning."

"Yeah, I just came to get a glass of water."

"Here, I'll get it for you."

"I'm perfectly capable of getting my own water, Tucker."

"I know you are, but there's nothing wrong with letting someone who's closer to the glasses and the sink do something for you, Rach."

Rachel didn't know what to say to that, even when he handed her the glass of water. So she could only take it, and head back upstairs, with those words turning over in her head.

TUCK WAS NOT in a great mood. Usually when he felt this edgy, he kept himself far away from his family. He wouldn't take his temper out on anyone. Ace Wyatt might be his father, but he didn't have to be like the man. He got to choose who he was and how he treated people.

He was very afraid he wouldn't treat anyone very nicely in this mood, and quite unfortunately he had to deal with Wyatts and Knights all day long.

Tuck hated lying to his brothers. He didn't relish lying to the Knights, either, and last night with Rachel he'd felt like a jerk. She was afraid for Duke and Tucker knew he was fine, but couldn't tell her.

Then there was that odd reaction to touching her bare shoulders and inappropriately noticing that Rachel's pajamas were not exactly *modest*…

Nope. He wasn't thinking about that. Rachel was and always had been off-limits. Him and Brady had always felt like any attraction to a Knight girl was disrespectful to Duke. A good, upstanding man, great rancher, excellent, loving father, helpful and compassionate neighbor. Next to Jamison, Duke had been the Wyatt brothers' paragon of what a man should be.

Of course, Brady had broken that personal rule. Now here he was, in love with Cecilia. Planning a future together once they were healed.

Tucker shook his head. Brady might be the most strict rule follower Tucker knew, but that didn't mean Brady slipping up on one personal tenant meant Tucker would. Or could.

He focused on the fact Brady was coming up to the Knight house, which no doubt meant Tucker was in store for a lecture from his older brother.

"You look rough," Brady commented, limping toward the porch where Tucker was standing, trying to get his temper under control.

"Yeah, you, too," he replied, then immediately winced. Brady had been shot in the leg just last month. He'd made great strides—this wound healing a lot quicker than his previous gunshot wound had.

Because Brady had been beaten to hell and back over the course of this dangerous summer, and what had Tucker done? Not a damn thing. "I updated Cody."

"I'm not here for an update." He took the stairs

with the help of his cane. "I'm here to see Cecilia before she heads in to the rez."

"Shouldn't she be going to you?"

"Walking is part of my physical therapy, Tuck," Brady replied mildly, standing in front of him and putting all his weight on one leg. "What crawled up your butt?"

Tucker scraped his hands over his face. "Running on no sleep. Sorry. Dev's out with Sarah, but I've got to stick close for Rachel. Making me a little antsy."

"How are you going to stick around when you've got work?"

"I've got a call with the sheriff this morning about doing some remote work, and leaving field work to Bligh for the time being."

His brother frowned. "I can help out around here. Just because of the bum leg doesn't mean I can't be of some use."

Tucker could easily read Brady's frustration with being out of commission. He couldn't imagine the feelings of futility, especially since Brady had been dealing with months of healing, not just weeks. "A lot of it's just research and following leads from the computer. Once I've got a decent thread to tug on, I'll share it with you." Which ignored the fact his brother could help with the watching out around the ranch, but Tuck didn't want to go there.

Brady nodded, then studied him a little too closely for Tuck's comfort. "I'm trusting you, Tuck." He nodded toward the house. "I always have. It hasn't changed."

Tucker shoved his hands in his pockets. He knew Brady was referencing last month when Tucker had called in backup to get Brady and Cecilia out of a dangerous situation. There'd been some aspects of that rescue mission that Tucker had had to lie about to keep his involvement with North Star a secret, and he knew Cecilia hadn't trusted him at all. But when push had come to shove, Brady had. It meant a lot. "Well, good. You should."

"I haven't said anything, and I won't. But maybe you could talk to Cody…"

Tucker couldn't let him finish his sentence, since he had a feeling it was about North Star. "This is my thing, Brady. Let it go."

Brady opened his mouth to say something, but the door behind them swung open.

"I thought I heard you." Cecilia came out in her tribal police uniform, smiling at Brady. She crossed to Brady first, gave him a kiss.

Tucker looked away from the easy affection. It wasn't that it bothered him. His brothers deserved that kind of good in their lives, and if they were happy, Tuck didn't have any problem with their choice of significant other.

He just didn't really want to…*watch* it. It caused some uncomfortable itch. At first when Jamison and Cody had hooked up with their ex-girlfriends, both Knight fosters, he hadn't felt it. But something about Gage and Brady falling for Felicity and Cecilia respectively made things…weird.

Rachel stepped out onto the porch, and Tucker's

gut tightened with discomfort. Something he *refused*
to acknowledge when it came to Duke's daughter
who was a good eight years younger than him.

"Who all needs breakfast? I'm making omelets."

"I got fifteen minutes before I need to head out,"
Cecilia said. She patted Brady's stomach. "Don't tell
me you actually snuck away from Grandma Pauline
without getting stuffed full of breakfast."

"Mak was doing his crawling demonstration.
Grandma was distracted, so I made a run for it."
He had his arm casually wrapped around Cecilia's
waist. An easy unit where one hadn't been before.
They'd helped Cecilia's friend keep her infant son,
Mak, safe, and now both lived at Grandma Pauline's,
as well.

"All right. Tucker, since you're our sudden houseguest, you can come help me with setting the table."
Rachel smiled sunnily, then turned back into the
house.

Cecilia and Brady's gazes were on him, a steady,
disapproving unit.

"Whatever is going on, she needs to stay far, far
away from it," Cecilia said solemnly. "I'll give you
the space to handle it, Tuck, because it seems that
whatever's going on needs that, but I'm holding you
personally responsible if anything happens to Rachel."

"She's not so helpless as all that," Tucker replied,
trying not to let his discomfort, or the weight of those
words, show.

"You know what I mean, whether you admit you do or not. Now you better get in there and help out."

Tucker had a few things to say in response, but he'd get nowhere against these two hardheads. Better to just save his breath. He had enough of a fight ahead of him—he'd just avoid the ones that were pointless.

He stepped into the kitchen as Rachel sprinkled a ham, cheese and pepper mixture into a pan.

"Let me guess, Cecilia was saying how you need to watch out for me or she's going to leave you in the middle of the Badlands chained to a rock with no water."

Tucker couldn't help but smile—at both the colorful specificity and how well she understood Cecilia. "It was a little less violent than all that, but the general gist."

"I don't need to be babied."

"Believe it or not, that's what I told her."

Rachel made a considering sound and said nothing else, so Tucker set out plates and silverware. He couldn't understand why she was cooking for everyone. "Why do you go to all this trouble?"

"It isn't any trouble to make breakfast."

"You and Grandma Pauline. Cereal isn't good enough. A frozen pizza is an affront. I happen to subsist just fine off of both when I'm at my apartment."

"That's because you have us to come home to."

Come home to. He didn't know why those words struck him as poignant. Of course, Grandma Pauline's was home. It was the place he'd grown up after escaping the Sons. It was the first place he'd been safe and loved.

"I guess you're right."

"Grandma Pauline taught me that you can't solve anyone's problems, but you can make them comfortable while they solve their own."

"What about when *you* have problems?"

She paused, then expertly flipped an omelet onto a plate next to her. "We aren't the ones out fighting the bad guys," Rachel said, and he could tell she was picking her words carefully.

"That doesn't mean you're without problems."

She inhaled sharply, working on the next omelet with ease and skill, but she didn't say anything to that.

Like Grandma Pauline, she was so often at the stove it seemed a part of her. Yet she'd been blinded at the age of three, lost her mother at the age of seven. Maybe she hadn't survived a ruthless biker gang like he had, but she had been scarred. Now he had to stay under the same roof as her and *lie*.

Not just to protect her, though. He was also protecting Duke, and the life he'd built. As long as North Star brought him back in one piece, did the lies matter?

Still, he stood frozen, watching her finish up the omelets, as Cecilia and Brady strolled in, still with their arms around each other. A few moments later, Sarah and Dev came in from the fields, bickering with the dogs weaving between them.

The North Star worked in secrets, in following the mission regardless of feelings, and he'd made a promise when he'd signed on with them. He wouldn't break it.

But it was a promise to be here, to be part of these families, too. He couldn't break that, either.

So he had to find a compromise.

Chapter Five

Conversation around the breakfast table flowed the way it always did when Wyatts and Knights got together. Rapid-fire subject changes, people talking over each other, Sarah and Dev constantly disagreeing with each other.

They avoided the topic of Duke, though it hung over them like a black cloud. Still, Rachel appreciated how hard they all tried to make it seem as though this were normal. In a way it was. They'd eaten hundreds of meals together over the years. Usually not in her kitchen, though.

"You going to eat that, Tuck?" Sarah asked through a mouthful of omelet.

Rachel frowned. Why wouldn't Tucker be eating? "I can make you a different kind if you'd like."

"No, it's fine."

She heard the scrape of fork on plate and was sure Tucker had just taken a large bite. He needed to eat. He hadn't slept, that much she'd known when she'd woken up and there'd been coffee before Sarah had even come down.

"I'm just thinking," he continued. "Something about this whole Duke thing doesn't...match."

Whatever chatter had been going on around the table faded into silence at the mention of her father. Rachel's appetite disappeared and she set down her fork.

"Duke left of his own accord," Tucker continued. "Maybe he's being blackmailed in some way, but he left on his own two feet. With everything that's happened this summer, I'd assume it has to do with the Sons, but there's no evidence that it does."

"What else could it have to do with?" Cecilia demanded.

"That's what doesn't jive. Maybe there's something in Duke's background we're missing."

Dad's *background*. "Just what exactly are you suggesting about my father?"

"Nothing bad, Rach. Just that there's more to the story than we've got."

"I don't see how we can rule out the Sons," Cecilia returned. "Not when four of Duke's foster daughters are hooked up with four of Ace's sons."

"I'm not saying rule it out. You can never rule out the Sons. I'm saying, look beyond them, too. Look at *Duke*. Not just where he's gone, but why. He wasn't taken. His house wasn't set on fire. This is different than the times the Knights have been caught in the crossfire of the Sons."

Rachel heard the voice from her nightmare echo in her head. Silly. It was just a dream, and it had nothing to do with what Tucker was talking about.

"What could Duke be hiding? We've been underfoot forever," Sarah said. "Wouldn't we know if he had some deep dark secret?"

Secrets always hurt the innocent.

Rachel squeezed her eyes shut, trying to push the dream out of her head. It had no bearing on the actual real conversation in front of her. That voice was made up, born of stress and worry and an overactive imagination.

She stood and pushed away from the table, abruptly taking her plate to the sink.

"Rach—" But Cecilia was cut off by someone's phone going off.

Cecilia muttered a curse. "I have to get to work."

There was the scraping of chairs, Dev and Sarah arguing over what work they had to get back to, Brady offering thanks for the breakfast as he left with Cecilia. The voices faded away, punctuated by the squeak and slap of the screen door.

And though he didn't make any noise, Rachel knew Tucker was still there. Likely watching her as she cleaned up the breakfast mess.

"Do you have something to say?" she demanded irritably, which wasn't like her. Nothing about the past week or so felt like *her*. She wanted to yell and rage and punch somebody and make her life go back to the way it was.

Weren't you just complaining about your life staying forever the same?

Rachel stopped washing the pan she'd used to cook the omelets and let out a pained breath. She'd wanted change, yes, but on her terms. Not the kind of change that put her father in danger.

"Did something I say upset you?" Tucker asked carefully. Like she was fragile and needed careful tiptoeing around.

"Do you assume everything is about you? That's pretty self-centered of you."

He was quiet for a long time, then she could hear him stacking dishes and placing them next to her so she could finish loading the dishwasher.

"It's just a theory, that this has something to do with Duke and not the Sons. It's not the only theory. I'm just struggling to find any evidence that ties to the Sons."

"I'm sure that struggle has nothing to do with how little you want to tie your father's gang to my father's disappearance."

"Don't be a child, Rachel," he snapped, with enough force to make her jolt. And to feel shamed.

"I wasn't—"

"I'm more aware of everything my father has done than you'll ever know. He's also in maximum-security prison because my brothers put their lives on the line to make it so. And so did some of your sisters. Let's not pretend I'm under any delusion that I could ever erase the effect my father has had on your family, through no fault of your family's."

The shame dug deeper, infusing her face with heat. "I'm sorry. I didn't mean—"

"You meant to slap at me, and I get it. You want to take out your fear and your frustration on me and

I'm usually a pretty good target. But not today. So back off."

Fully chastened, Rachel reached out. She found his arm and gave it a squeeze. "I am sorry."

She could hear him sigh as he patted her hand. "I am, too. I didn't sleep worth a darn, and I'm not handling it well."

Silence settled over them, her fingers still wrapped around his arm, his big hand resting over hers. It was warm and rough. Despite being a detective, Tucker helped out at the ranch as much as he could, which was probably where he'd gotten the callouses. The big hands were just a family trait. All the Wyatts were big. She was a tall woman, but Tucker's hands still dwarfed hers. If she flipped her hand over, so they were palm to palm—

Why was she thinking about that? She pulled her hand away from under his, and only the fact she was at the sink kept her from backing away. She had dishes to finish, so she turned back to them, ignoring the way her body was all…jittery all of a sudden.

"My theory about Duke seemed to upset you," he said, in a tone she would have considered his detective voice. Deceivingly casual as he tried to get deeper information on a topic. "Do you know something about what's going on? About Duke's past?"

She laughed, with a bitterness she couldn't seem to shove away. "No, I don't know anything."

"You're acting like you do."

She blew out a breath. Mr. Detective wasn't letting it go, so she had to be honest with him even if it was embarrassing. "I had one of those nightmares last night that felt real. I can't seem to shake it."

"Why don't you tell it to me?"

She shook her head. How embarrassing to lay out her silly, childish dreams for him to hear. He'd tell her they were natural. She'd had a traumatic experience as a young child and her brain was still dealing with it and blah, blah, blah.

"Grandma Pauline always said if you explain your nightmare, it takes away its power."

She couldn't help but smile at that. Grandma Pauline had something to say about everything, and wasn't that a comfort? "Did that work?"

He was quiet for a minute. "With the things that weren't real."

The word *real* lodged in her chest like a pickax. Sharp. Painful. Both because Tuck probably had plenty of real nightmares after almost eight years raised in a terrible biker gang, and because hers wasn't real. No matter how much it felt that way. "It wasn't real," she insisted.

"Then lay it on me."

TUCKER HAD NEVER seen Rachel quite so...wound up. He understood this situation was stressful, but they'd been in stressful situations all summer, and she'd kept her cool.

Did she know something? Was the dream some kind of distraction? Something wasn't adding up.

He'd brought up Duke's past because it was a possible answer. If Brady or Cecilia stumbled upon those facts on their own, without him telling them specifically what, then he wouldn't have betrayed his promise to North Star.

They probably wouldn't see it that way, but the more he felt the need to comfort Rachel as she came slowly unraveled, the less he cared about North Star's approval.

They'd put him in an impossible situation. All because he wanted to do what was right. Well, getting some of his own answers was right.

Rachel hesitated as she did the dishes. Finally, she shrugged. "It's silly. I just… I've always had nightmares about the night I was attacked by that mountain lion."

"That makes sense."

"It does. Usually they're few and far between. Especially as I've grown up. But something about the last few weeks has made them an almost nightly occurrence, and they're morphing from memory into fiction. But the fiction feels more real than the memory." She frowned, eyebrows drawing together and a line appearing across her forehead.

She really was beautiful in her own right. Much as she could remind him of Eva, the older she got, the more she was just… Rachel. He knew her sisters sometimes saw her as the baby of the family, the sweet girl with no grit, but that was her power. A softer Grandma Pauline, she held everyone together. Not with a wooden spoon, but with her calm, caring demeanor.

And *why* was he thinking about that? He should

be thinking about what she was saying. "Well, what's different? Between the real dream and the fiction dream?"

She took a deep breath and let it out slowly. She looked so troubled that he wanted to reach out and hold her hand. He curled his fingers into his palm instead. Touching seemed…dangerous lately.

"Instead of a mountain lion, there's a man. He has blue eyes, and half his face is scarred. Not like mine. Not lines, but all over. Like a burn, sort of. He's carrying me. We're…" Her eyebrows drew together again, like she was struggling to remember. "It was the hills in one of the pastures. I don't know which one, but that's where the mountain lion attack happened. Outside one of the pastures."

"Do you remember if that's where the mountain lion attack happened or is that just what you've been told?"

She stopped rinsing a plate. "What does it matter?"

"For the purpose of your dream. Is that part real— what you actually remember when you're awake. Or is it what you've been told so that's what your subconscious shows you?"

"I… I guess I'm not sure." She put the plate in the dishwasher then turned to him.

He'd hoped getting it off her chest would ease her mind some, but she seemed just as twisted up. Like the more she talked about it, the more it didn't add up.

"Mom and Dad didn't like to talk about it, but I remember sometimes they'd mention something and it didn't…match with what I thought had happened. But I was only three. Their memory would be more accurate."

"Okay, so in your dream the mountain lion usually takes you somewhere?"

"No. I'm already there. He jumps out of nowhere. I see the glint of something sharp and then I wake up before it swipes at me. But…the dream last night was more involved. I was being carried away. The man's talking. And the thing glinting in the moonlight isn't claws. It's some kind of knife."

She whirled away abruptly. "It's a *nightmare*, Tuck. It's happening when I'm asleep. It's nothing and I'm tired of it making me feel so unsettled."

He watched her agitated pacing, decided to hold his tongue and let her get it out. Maybe she needed a full-on breakdown to be able to find that center of calm that was so inherent to her.

"But I can't get that *fictional* man's voice out of my head. The way he talks. There's an accent. Like New York or Boston. Why is that so clear to me? What can't I shake this stupid dream?"

She raked her fingers through her hair, and Tucker desperately wanted to offer her some soothing words and a hug, but over the past day any physical offers of comfort had gone a little weird. He needed to keep his hands to himself.

"Secrets always hurt the innocent." She dropped her hands, wrapping them around her body instead. "I keep hearing this voice say that. *Secrets always hurt the innocent. Curtis Washington is going to learn that the hard way."*

Tucker's entire body went cold. He didn't know that name, but having a specific name, a specific voice in her dreams...

Dread skittered up his spine.

"Who's Curtis Washington?"

"I don't know. I've never heard that name before. It's just in my head."

Tucker had to work to keep his breathing even. To maintain control and a neutral expression rather than let all his theories run away from him in a jumble of worry.

She gestured toward him. "Say something."

He had to be careful about his words. About how he approached this horrible possibility. "Mountain lions aren't particularly aggressive."

"No, but I was three. Who knew what I was doing."

"You were three. Why were you so far from your parents? Duke and Eva weren't exactly hands-off parents."

"They...they didn't like to talk about it. I probably wandered off. Accidentally. Not because they weren't paying attention. You know how toddlers are. It's possible... It just happened."

She didn't seem so sure.

"This voice...this man..."

"It's stupid. All my life the dream has been a mountain lion. The man is a recent change, Tuck. It's a new morph on the old nightmare. If something else happened that night, why would I only dream about it now?"

Because Duke was in trouble, in danger. And this was his WITSEC life. Which meant he had another name.

Could it be the name in Rachel's dream?

Chapter Six

Tucker made himself scarce after Rachel had told him her dream. She could hardly blame him. Why was she coming so unglued over a nightmare? It made no sense, and if it was irritating to her—she could only imagine how annoying it was to the people around her.

She wouldn't bring it up ever again. Not to Tucker, not to anyone. Her dreams were her problem.

She went through the rest of the day without seeing him, though she knew he was there. Then he popped in for dinner, chatting cheerfully though she could tell he was distracted. He helped clean up after dinner, then he disappeared into Dad's room.

Door shut.

She had to admit, she didn't feel babysat, even though that's why he was here. Still, it helped that he wasn't hovering. Which meant she had the space inside herself to recognize Sarah's irritation simmering off her in its usual fraught waves.

Rachel had never been to the ocean, but she always associated Sarah's moods with the slapping waves and whipping winds of a hurricane.

While Sarah's moods were often operatic in nature, Rachel couldn't blame her right now. She was carrying the entire ranch on her shoulders, even with Dev's help.

"How about an ice-cream sundae?"

"I'm not a child, Rach," Sarah replied grumpily. But Rachel heard her plop herself at the kitchen table.

Rachel got out all the fixings for a sundae. Her conversation with Tucker from breakfast repeated in her mind.

Grandma Pauline taught me that you can't solve anyone's problems, but you can make them comfortable while they solve their own.

What about when you have problems?

She supposed her comfort was making other people food, and she supposed she'd gotten that from Grandma Pauline. She'd never fully realized how much she'd adopted the older woman's response to stress or fear, or wondered why before.

It wasn't hard to put together, though. Grandma Pauline was the last word around here. You didn't cross her, but everyone loved and respected her. They spoke about Grandma Pauline with reverence or loving humor.

"What do you think about what Tucker said?" Sarah asked.

Rachel blinked, remembering she was supposed to be making a sundae. Heck, she'd make one for herself, too. "Which part?"

"This being more about Dad than the Sons?"

Rachel scooped the ice cream, poured on chocolate syrup and sprayed on some whipped cream. She set one bowl in front of Sarah, then took her seat at the table with her own bowl.

They were the two youngest Knight girls, often sheltered from danger. Not just because they were the youngest or because Rachel was blind, but because they hadn't come from the dire circumstances their sisters had. Rachel had been born happy and healthy to Duke and Eva, their miracle baby. Sarah had been adopted at birth, so Sarah didn't remember or know anything about her birth parents.

Neither Rachel nor Sarah had ever left home. No tribal police or park ranger jobs for them. Rachel's part-time job as an art teacher was a challenge, and Sarah being a rancher was definitely hard work, but they were home. Still sheltered from so much of the *bad* in the world.

So, if Rachel could be honest with anyone, it was Sarah, because more than everyone else they were especially in this together. "I really don't know what to think of it."

"He's a detective," Sarah said.

"It doesn't make him infallible."

"No, but it gives him some experience in putting clues together. He also knows the Sons, and much as I hate to agree with Dev, he's right. The Sons have left Duke alone for all this time." Her sister released a breath. "So why would they start poking at him now?

Especially with Ace in jail. Ace is the one with the vendetta against the Wyatts, not the Sons in general."

"I don't imagine they feel kindly toward the boys who escaped, or the men who put their leader in jail."

"Maybe not. I'm not saying it can't possibly be the Sons. God knows almost all our problems this summer have come from that corner of the scummy world. But… Dad never talks about his parents."

Rachel frowned at that. Surely that wasn't true. But no, she couldn't remember any stories about Dad's parents.

"It never really dawned on me that it was weird since we had Grandma and Grandpa Mills. And I always *assumed* this ranch was passed down, Knight to Knight, because Dad's so proud of it, but…wouldn't there be stories? Heirlooms?"

"What are you trying to say?" Rachel demanded, panic clutching at her.

"We don't actually know anything about Dad, and we never asked. As far as stories I've heard, and just being around Dad, his life started when he met Mom. And that can't be true."

Rachel couldn't eat another bite of ice cream. What was there curdled in her stomach. Sarah was right. She couldn't think of a thing Dad had ever told her about his life before he'd met her mother.

"So, you think he's running from something in his past?"

"Or running *to* something in his past."

Rachel thought of the gun under his pillow. About Dad not wanting her teaching. "He didn't want me to teach this session. He blamed it on the trouble with the Wyatts, but I taught all summer through all that danger."

"So, he was afraid. Something was *making* him afraid. I can't imagine Dad leaving us if he thought we were in danger. Unless…"

"Unless what?" Rachel demanded.

"What if he did something wrong? What if there isn't danger so much as… I mean, he could have run away from something bad."

"Dad would never. He wouldn't… No, I don't believe that."

"He wouldn't have left us in danger, Rachel. So one of these things he would never do *has* to be what he's done."

What a horrible, horrible thought. Maybe it was true, and maybe she was naive, but she refused to believe it of the father she loved. This man who had been a shining example of goodness and hardworking truth. "What if he thought only he was in danger? Just like Cecilia and Brady when they were trying to save Mak. They thought staying here would bring trouble to our doorstep, so they took off trying to draw the danger with them."

Sarah didn't respond to that. They sat in silence for ticking minutes.

"We have to tell Tucker he was right," her sister finally said. "That we don't know anything about his life before Mom. The answer is somewhere in there, and Tuck can find it. He's a detective. He has to be able to find it."

Rachel wasn't so sure. If her father had kept this secret for over thirty years, maybe no one could find it.

"Rach." Sarah's hand grasped hers across the table. "We have to help in whatever way we can. We're always swept off to the sidelines. But who put out that fire last month? We did. Who always holds down the fort? Us. And we're damn good at it. But Dad's gone. He can't protect us like he's always trying to do. Whether he's running away or hiding or *whatever*, it's just us. We have to step up to the plate."

Rachel knew Sarah was right, and she didn't understand the bone-deep reticence inside of her. It felt like they were stirring up trouble that would change *everything*, and she didn't want everything to change. Maybe she'd wanted a *little* change, but not her whole world.

"I can talk to Tucker myself. If you don't want to—"

"No…you're right. It's just us. We have to work together. It's the only way to make sure Dad's safe."

"He's a tough old bird," Sarah said firmly, and Rachel knew she was comforting herself as much as trying to comfort Rachel.

"He is. And we'll bring him home."

TUCKER CALLED EVERY North Star number he had in his arsenal over the course of the day, and no one would answer. He was too annoyed to be worried that was a bad sign. He needed to know if Curtis Washington was Duke's real name.

It would change things. For North Star, too. He

barked out another irritable message into Granger's voice mail, then threw his phone on the bed in disgust.

He'd searched Duke's room, too. No hints to a secret past. There'd been plenty of guns secreted throughout the room, which led Tucker to believe Duke was a man who'd known his past would catch up with him eventually.

No. He'd fostered five girls, raised one daughter of his own. Duke had been certain he'd left that old life behind. Something must have recently happened to lead him to believe he was in danger.

And it tied to the Sons. It shouldn't make Tucker feel guilty. Just because he'd been born into the Sons didn't make him part of them. His life had nothing to do with Duke's secret past.

But the guilt settled inside of him anyway. Luckily, a knock sounded at the door and he could pretend he didn't feel it.

"Come in," he offered.

Sarah poked her head in. "Hey, can we talk to you in the kitchen for a second?"

"Uh, sure."

He followed her out of the room and down the hall. Rachel was already in the kitchen, washing out some bowls. He wondered if she ever stepped away from that constant need to cook and clean for everyone. He wondered if anyone offered a hand, and doubted it very much. He knew from experience how little kitchen work held appeal after a long day ranching.

Maybe that explained it. This was her way of helping her family, the ranch. It was how she felt useful.

When she heard them enter, she turned and
smiled. "Did you want some dessert?"

"No, thanks. What did you want to talk about?"

Rachel took a seat at the table, but Sarah paced,
wringing her hands together. "We were thinking
about what you said. About Duke's life, and the truth
is…" She looked at Rachel, so Tucker did, too.

Her expression was carefully blank, calm, which
told him all he needed to know. Inside, she was anything but.

"We don't know anything about his life before he
married Mom," Sarah continued. "He never talked
about parents or siblings. Where he was born or if
this ranch was passed on. We just…assumed. And
we had so much family, and everything with losing
Mom, and Liza and Nina disappearing and… Well,
you know. It just didn't come up. Until now."

Liza's stay with the Knights had been brief, but
her returning to the Sons had hurt all of the Knights,
and Jamison. Liza and Jamison had since patched
things up after saving Liza's half sister, but it had
taken a long time.

Nina's disappearing had been the only time in
Tucker's life where he thought Duke might actually
cut all ties with the Wyatts. He'd personally blamed
Tucker's youngest brother Cody, Nina's boyfriend
at the time. It had taken a long time for Duke to get
past it. When Nina had returned—injured and with
her daughter in tow—Tucker had been sure Duke

would be furious all over again, but the reconciliation of Cody and Nina had soothed some of his anger.

Some.

There was the guilt again, darker this time. Tucker *knew* Duke had a secret life. He'd put the idea in their heads. Now he was going to lie to them as if he didn't know what it was.

Where does your loyalty lie? North Star or your friends?

Two very different women stared at him. Rachel, dark hair, eyes and skin. Tall and slender. Sarah, petite, curvy, with baby blues and flyaway blond hair.

He wanted to tell them the truth. He couldn't think of a good reason not to, except Granger had told him not to. Duke hadn't argued with it. There might be a very good reason Sarah and Rachel should be kept in the dark.

What might they do if they knew the truth?

"I'm…looking into it. His past, that is. Best I can. To see if it connects to anything that's going on." He did his best not to cringe, not to show how utterly slimy he felt for the flat-out lies. "I haven't gotten very far because I don't have a lot to go on. I don't suppose you have any ideas?"

Sarah shook her head sadly. "That's just it. Who *never* talks about their parents? Or where they're from. Dad's got to be from South Dakota. How else would he end up with all this?"

Tucker really hated that he knew the answer to that question. He forced himself to smile reassuringly. "I'll keep digging. I—"

He was interrupted by his phone going off. It wasn't his regular ringtone. He frowned at the screen. It must be a North Star number. "I have to take this," he said, pushing away from the table.

Both women looked at him with frowns, but he lifted the phone to his ear and stepped out of the kitchen. "Wy—"

Granger was barking out questions before Tucker even got his last name out of his mouth. "Where'd you get that name?"

Tucker felt shattered, and he didn't even fully understand why. He looked back at the kitchen. No one had followed, but he still slid into Duke's room and closed the door. "So, it's true. That's his real name."

Why was Rachel dreaming about Duke's real name? A man instead of a mountain lion?

"I asked where you got the name, Wyatt."

Tucker hesitated. He had the sinking suspicion if he mentioned it was in Rachel's dream, she'd be dragged into this. Maybe North Star would keep her safe. Maybe they even needed to know that she knew something. But…

He couldn't bring himself to utter her name. It felt wrong, and beyond that, he doubted very much Duke wanted his daughter dragged into this even if she did know something.

And his loyalty *was* to his friends over the North Star Group. Even if they were doing something good in trying to take down the Sons, and that *was* important. But so was safeguarding Rachel.

So, he lied instead. "I did some research on dirty

cops in Chicago. You did give me enough information to go on to make an educated guess."

"Wyatt. Your job is to keep your families from getting suspicious while we handle the real threat. I don't need any misdirected people wading into this. Keep your side out of it. No more digging. Do you understand me?"

Tucker wanted to say *or what*, but he had a feeling Granger McMillan was dangerous enough to make *or what* hurt. "All right, but it seems to me it'd be more helpful if I knew the whole story."

"I don't need your help. I need you to keep your families out of it. That's it. If you can't do that, I'll bring in someone who can, and you will be dealt with accordingly."

Tucker opened his mouth to tell Granger to jump off a cliff, but the line went dead.

Probably for the best. He let out a long breath.

Rachel knew her father's real name without knowing that's what it was. Which meant, she'd had *some* encounter with *someone* who'd been a part of Duke's previous life.

If that someone was still out there, if that someone was behind this connection to the Sons, it meant Rachel was as much of a target as Duke.

Chapter Seven

Rachel didn't have the dream. She woke up feeling rested for the first time in days. It might have put her in a good mood, but as long as her father was missing, there was no real good mood to have.

Tucker had promised to look into Duke's past, but she had to wonder if it wouldn't end up being… catastrophic somehow. She didn't want to believe her father was involved in something bad, but how could she ignore facts?

He'd left of his own accord, sort of. She still believed he'd been forced to leave, but he hadn't been carted off or held at gunpoint. His little disappearing act and fake vacation *had* to be born out of threats, or something like that.

Rachel got dressed, trying to remind herself there wasn't anything she could do about it. She had to trust Tucker and the Wyatts to look into her father's disappearance. And Cecilia. Cecilia wouldn't sit idly by. None of her sisters would. Sarah would ranch, Nina and Liza were busy with their children but would probably help Cody and Jamison in whatever ways they could. Felicity should be concentrating on growing her baby, but she would likely discuss with Gage what was going on.

And Rachel would be left to cook and clean. She tried not to be disgusted with herself. After all, if it was good enough for Grandma Pauline, it was good enough for her.

But Grandma Pauline was eighty. Rachel also had no doubt she'd pick up that big rifle she kept hidden in the pantry and take care of whatever intruders might deign to invade her ranch.

What could Rachel do? Scream?

No. That really wasn't good enough. She needed to learn some basics about getting away or fighting back.

She'd insist Tucker teach her. If he had to be underfoot, the least he could do was be useful. She headed downstairs and to her normal routine of making breakfast, but she stopped short at the entrance to the kitchen.

Tucker was in her kitchen. She couldn't tell what he was doing, but she could make out his outline. She could hear the sounds of…cooking.

"What are you doing?" she demanded, maybe a little too accusatorially to be fair.

"Thought I could take breakfast duty since I'm staying here," he replied, continuing to move around *her* kitchen as if she were just some sort of… bystander.

"But… I always make breakfast."

"Don't tell me you've completely morphed into

Grandma Pauline and can't stand someone else carrying some weight?"

"That isn't…" She had to trail off because it was silly to be upset someone had beaten her to breakfast. She'd been complaining for years that Duke and Sarah never even tried to figure out their way around the kitchen.

She should be grateful someone was lending a hand, even if it was Tucker. But mostly she felt incredibly superfluous and useless. "I guess I'll—"

"Have a seat. It's almost ready. I don't want you picking up after me. I can do my own laundry, keep Duke's room tidy and all that. I'm not your houseguest, so you don't need to treat me like one. I'm here to help. That's all."

"Being here to help does technically make you a guest," Rachel muttered irritably.

"Well, this guest can take care of himself." As if to prove it, he slid a plate in front of her. "All I did was bake some of Grandma's cinnamon rolls you had in the freezer and cut up a melon. Hardly putting myself out."

"But what if your coffee sucks?" she asked, trying to make light of how small that made her feel. When did she get so pathetic that she needed to make a meal to feel worthy of her spot here?

He slid the mug in front of her. "It doesn't. And, I already doctored it. You're welcome."

The coffee didn't suck. She might have made it a little stronger for Sarah, but he had indeed put in cream and sugar just how she liked it. She wanted to make a joke about keeping him around, but it sat uncomfortably on her chest so she couldn't form the words.

It was a little too easy to picture. She knew it would be…difficult to find a significant other. Not so much because of her scarring and lack of sight, but because she just didn't get around much and lived in a rural area. But she'd always had that little dream of a husband and kids in this kitchen.

To even picture Tucker filling that role was *embarrassing*. So she shoved a bite of cinnamon roll in her mouth instead. Even after being frozen, Grandma Pauline's cinnamon rolls were like a dream.

"You know, Sarah and Duke would mess up even reheating frozen rolls," she offered, trying to think of anything else than what was currently occupying her brain.

He took the seat next to her, presumably with his own plate of food and mug of coffee. "If that's what you want to tell yourself, Rach, but I don't think you give them much space to figure out how."

She frowned at that.

"I'm sorry," he said. "I wasn't trying to be a jerk. Maybe you're right and they can't."

But she could tell he didn't think so, and worse she knew he was right. She complained about how little they did, while never ever giving them even an inch to do it for themselves.

She ate her feelings via one too many cinnamon rolls, then started on the fruit. She could wallow in…

well, everything, or she could do something. She could act. She could *change*.

"Tuck, I want you to teach me how to fight."

"Huh?"

"I can't shoot. But I could fight." She pushed the plate away, ignoring the last few bites of melon. "I want to be able to defend myself. Maybe nothing bad happens here, but I want to be ready if it does."

"Rach, you don't have to worry about that. We're all—"

"Tucker." She reached across the table, found his arm. She needed that connection to make sure he understood this was more than just…a suggestion. She needed it. Needed to feel like she could contribute or at least not make a situation worse. "I could fight. I want to be able to fight." She gave his arm a squeeze.

He hesitated, but he didn't immediately shoot her down again. "I'm sure Cecilia—"

"Isn't here. You are. Didn't you teach some self-defense class at the Y for a while?"

She could hear him shift in his chair, a sense of embarrassment almost. "Well, yeah, but—"

"But what? What's different about that and this?"

After a long beat of silence, he finally spoke. "I guess there really isn't one."

"Exactly. So, you'll do it." She didn't phrase it as a question, because she wasn't taking no for an answer.

"I guess I could teach you and Sarah a few things." He didn't sound enthused about it, but she'd take agreement with or without excitement.

Rachel heard Sarah stepping into the kitchen, and

then her small bright form entered Rachel's blurry vision.

"What things are you teaching me?"

"Self-defense. Rachel wants to learn how to fight."

Rachel noted that, while he didn't sound sure of teaching her anything, he didn't seem dismissive or disapproving. Maybe he didn't like teaching was all.

Well, he'd have to suck it up.

"Good idea," Sarah said around a mouthful of food. "But I can shoot a gun. And kick your butt, if I had to."

"Kick *my* butt?" Tucker replied incredulously. "You're five foot nothing. If that."

"I also wrestle stubborner cows than you, Wyatt. I could take you down right here, right now."

"All right." There was the scrape of the chair against the floor. "You're on."

"Oh, you don't want to mess with me."

Rachel could see the outlines of them circling each other. "You aren't really going to…"

There was the sound of a grunt, a thud and then laughter. It was a nice sound. Comforting. Like having her family home. Except Dad wasn't here, and they were pretending to fight.

"All right. Sarah gets a pass," Tucker conceded. "Though I maintain you did not kick my butt."

"Whatever you gotta tell yourself, Tuck," Sarah replied cheerfully. "Dev's truck is already out there." The cheer died out of her voice. "I could wring his neck. I told him to wait for me. Leave me a cinnamon roll to heat up," she called, already halfway out the door.

The door slammed.

"Did you let her win?" Rachel asked.

"It wasn't about winning. I just wanted to see what she's got. Good instincts and a nice jab. She's scrappy and mean, which is good in a real fight. Besides, she's right. She can shoot."

"Are you saying I'm not scrappy and mean?"

Tucker laughed. "I wasn't saying that, but we both know you're not. Which is why I'll teach you a few self-defense moves, if it'll make you feel better."

"It will. When do we start?"

Autumn in South Dakota meant anything could happen. A nice sunny day. A sudden blizzard. Today was a pleasant morning, thank God. The yard in front of the Knight house would be as good a place as any to teach Rachel a few moves.

Rachel had changed from jeans and a T-shirt to something…he couldn't think too much about. It was all stretchy and formfitting, so he kept his gaze firmly on the world around him and not on her.

"Shouldn't we have padding or something? I don't want to hurt you."

The fact she wasn't joking was somehow endearing. Before he'd moved to detective, he'd been on the road. Fought off the occasional person too high on drugs to feel pain, quite a few men larger and meaner than him, and more than one criminal with a weapon.

"We're just doing a few lessons. Learn a few rules

and moves. You're not going to be beating me up quite yet."

"But shouldn't I be able to?"

"Sure. But we'll have to work up to it. You can't learn everything there is to know about self-defense in a day."

She wrinkled her nose. "Is it *that* complicated?"

"It's not about being complicated. It's just…something you practice, so it becomes second nature. So you're ready to do it. But listen, Rach. You're not going to need to, because I'm here and—"

She shook her head. "I don't want to feel like the weak link. Like the person everyone has to protect. Maybe it isn't much, but I just want to be able to land a punch or get away from someone if I need to. That's all."

She more than deserved that. He just wished he didn't have to be the one to teach her. It would involve touching and guiding, and she was… Hell, exercise leggings and a stretchy top were not *fair*. He was *human*.

Human and better than his baser—and completely unacceptable—urges. Because he'd shaped himself into a good, honorable man. One who did not take advantage of a young woman who meant a lot to his family.

And to you.

Because what he could forget when he didn't spend too much time one-on-one with Rachel was that they had a lot in common. What she'd said inside about wanting to feel useful echoed inside of him.

Her surprise and irritation that he'd help out around the house made him want to do it all the more.

Take care of her and—

He cleared his throat, forced himself to focus. To treat this like any other lesson. "Rule number one. Always go for the crotch."

She made an odd sound. Like a strangled laugh. "I'm not going for your crotch, Tucker."

Jesus. He could *not* think about that. "Thanks for that. I just meant, in real life, that's your target. Crotch. Eyes. The most vulnerable points." He hated the thought of her needing to do *any* of that.

"Okay."

"You have to be mean."

She fisted her hands on her hips. "I know how to be mean."

"*Really* mean. Channel your inner Sarah."

"I'm going to channel my inner Grandma Pauline and whack you with a rolling pin."

Tucker laughed. "All right, killer. Show me how you'd punch."

He walked her through the proper form for a punch. Tried to talk her through aiming even though her sight was compromised. He instructed about grabbing anything she could make into a weapon. How to kick with the most effect.

Her form wasn't bad, and it got better the more she practiced. He offered to quit or take a break at least five times, but she kept wanting to go on. Even as they both ended up breathing heavily.

"The problem is I'm not going to be in a boxing

ring. If *I'm* going to be in a fight, it's probably going to be because someone's trying to hurt me or someone I love. But they'd underestimate me. Either by ignoring me or just grabbing me."

"Maybe, but you have to learn the basics."

"But I can practice punching and kicking form on my own. We need to practice like…how to get away if someone grabs me. I know you don't want to hurt me, and I don't want to hurt you, but it has to feel more like an actual fight."

"You don't have to worry about hurting me."

"Because I'm that weak?" she demanded.

"No, because I'm a professional at dodging a punch, Rach. I've been a cop for almost nine years. I've been learning to not get hit my whole life." He hadn't really meant to say that last part, or wouldn't have if he'd known she'd get that…sympathetic look on her face.

Nothing to be sympathetic about. He'd survived eight years of Ace Wyatt and the Sons of the Badlands. All his brothers, except Cody, had survived more time than him. Jamison hadn't gotten out until eighteen, after working hard to get Cody out before his seventh birthday. Tucker had followed not much later when he'd been eight. Gage and Brady had been eleven, and Dev twelve.

Tucker had gotten off easy, like he usually did.

She opened her mouth to say something—likely something he didn't want to hear, so he spoke first. "Come on then. If I'm coming at you, land a punch."

She got in the stance he'd taught her, made a good

fist. As he moved forward, she swung out. He easily pivoted so she didn't land it.

"That's good."

"I didn't hit you!"

Tucker laughed. "Don't sound so disappointed." He took her still-clenched hand by the wrist and held it up. "This is your dominant hand, so you want it to do the big work." He took her other hand and brought it up. "But this one needs to do the work, too. Make a fist."

He walked her through using both hands to punch. Using her arms to block. He let her land a few punches. She wasn't going to ward off any attackers with her fists—she'd have better luck kicking a vulnerable area or grabbing something to use as a weapon. Still, if it made her feel as though she was more prepared, that was what mattered.

It wasn't so bad all in all. It felt good to teach her something useful. A little *uncomfortable* teaching her to break holds by holding on to her against her will—but an important skill nonetheless.

Until he had the bright idea to teach her how to get away from someone who grabbed her from behind. Which necessitated…grabbing *her* from behind.

They went through the drill a few times. Slow, with pointers, and he tried very hard not to think about anything related to his body. He told her how to position her hands, how to maneuver her body. All while pretending his was made of…ice. Or plastic. Whatever kind of material that was not moved by a woman's body.

She was…lithe. Graceful.

Hot.

That was a really, really unacceptable thought when it came to Duke's daughter. Duke's daughter who's safety he was being entrusted with.

The strangest part was he'd scuffled with Sarah just this morning, and it hadn't felt any different than wrestling with his brothers. Familial. Funny.

But this was *none* of those things and he hadn't the slightest idea why.

"Do that again."

"I don't think—"

"Do it again," she insisted. "Come at me from behind."

He allowed himself to curse to his heart's content silently in his head. Rachel turned her back to him.

He just needed to enact a quick, meaningless grab around the waist.

The problem was he didn't like putting himself in the mind-set of an attacker. And he didn't like staying in his own mind-set, which was way too aware of how the exercise clothes she wore molded to every slender curve.

But who else could he be?

He gritted his teeth and tried to think about times tables as he wrapped his arm around her waist. She lifted her right hand to keep it from being held down by his grab, but he used his free hand to ensnare her arm.

She mimicked a kick to the insole and twisted in his grasp. He gave a little, as if stepping away from her kick. It gave her room, but kept his arm slightly around her, palm pressed to her stomach.

He wanted to tell her to pull her arm down in the way he'd shown her earlier, but he was afraid his voice wouldn't come out even. Or that he could manage to unclamp his jaw.

But she paused there, in this awkward position. His hand was on her abdomen, the fingers of his other hand curled around her wrist. He could feel the rise and fall of her breathing because her back was against him, her butt nestled way too close to a part of him he could *not* think about right now.

She tilted her head, and though he knew she couldn't see out of one eye and only general shapes out of the other, it felt as though she were studying him.

And then there was her mouth. Full and tempting. She wasn't trying to get out of his grasp, and she definitely wasn't putting any distance between their bodies.

She smelled like a meadow, and everything they were doing faded away. There were two aches inside of him—one he fully understood, and one that didn't make any sense. They both grew, expanded until there was only his heartbeat and the exhale of her breath across his cheek.

The sound of people arguing interrupted the buzzing in his head. He dropped her abruptly, moving away clumsily.

"Tucker…"

He didn't like the soft way she spoke, or the way

her breath shuddered in and out, or that look in her eye, which he could not in any circumstances think about or consider.

"Hey, there's Sarah and Dev. We've been at this a while, huh? How about a break? I'm starved, you know?"

Sweet hell he was *babbling*. He cleared his throat. He was a grown man. A grown man with an inappropriate attraction, but that just meant he knew what to do with it. Scurrying away and babbling were not it. Getting himself together and *handling* it was what he needed to do. Would do. Absolutely. *Obviously.*

The dogs raced over first, so Tucker focused on them, squatting to scratch them both behind their ears. He spoke to them in soothing tones and tried his damnedest to get that *ache* coursing around inside of him to dissipate.

"How goes the self-defense?" Sarah asked.

"Great," Tucker said, far too loudly. "Going to take a break now."

"Yeah, us, too."

When Tucker looked up, Dev was frowning at him, but Tucker reminded himself that his brother's resting face was frowning disapproval. That was all.

Besides, he had enough frowning disapproval for himself. He didn't need anyone else's.

Chapter Eight

Rachel went through the rest of the day with an odd…buzz along her skin. Like the precursor to getting poison ivy. It was uncomfortable. Not quite so painful as a rash, but uncomfortable. Definitely.

She knew it was all Tucker's fault. Though she couldn't figure out why. Had he read her mind? He had been horrified that she'd kind of enjoyed him manhandling her. Or, had he enjoyed manhandling her and was horrified?

Either way, there was some horror. And then locking it all away and acting his usual genial self.

Except that he avoided her at all costs.

Which was probably for the best. Or was it? She got ready for bed, edgy and worked up. There was just too much going on. Her father was missing. She was having recurring nightmares. She was apparently attracted to a man she'd always looked at as family. Sort of. And worse than being attracted to *him* was the wondering if he was attracted to her right back. Or oblivious.

She groaned and flopped onto her bed. She

needed to talk to someone. With most problems, she confided in Sarah or Cecilia. Sarah would be no help with this one, and Cecilia… She'd be too blunt. Too…forthright.

Rachel needed someone with a softer touch. So she called Felicity.

"Hey, Rach. Everything okay?"

"Yeah. Nothing new to report on our end."

Felicity sighed. "I really hate all this waiting. Gage keeps fluttering around me, trying to distract me from my stress, but all he is doing is stressing me out even more."

Rachel smiled. That was sweet. And also the perfect segue. "How did you end up involved with Gage?"

"What kind of question is that?"

"Not a mean one. I just… I wondered." Rachel rolled her eyes at herself. She sounded like an idiot. A transparent one. But at least of all her sisters, Felicity would never call her on it.

"Is this about Tucker?"

Rachel forced out a laugh. She was afraid it sounded more like a deranged array of squeaks. "What? No."

"You're a terrible liar. And even if you weren't, this is completely transparent."

Rachel pouted in spite of herself. "Of course it is. But you weren't supposed to call me out on it!"

Felicity laughed. "Sorry. Normally I wouldn't, but you're strung tight. I know Dad's whole disappearing act is scary, but you're usually calm in the midst of a crisis."

"I'm calm." Aside from the dreams. Aside from Tucker *touching* her. "Tucker believes Dad left of his own accord. Whatever prompted it, he doesn't think he's in any immediate danger and I have to believe that."

"I do, too. And so does Gage for that matter." Felicity paused. "So…why are you wound up?"

Rachel could blame it on the dreams. Some of it *was* the dreams, and the possibility of Dad being… far more complicated than she wanted him to be. But she didn't want to lay either of those things at Felicity's feet, where she'd worry needlessly.

"I think there was a moment. With Tucker. When he was teaching me some self-defense moves."

"Define *moment*."

"I don't know. Like…like…an awareness of each other. As a man and a woman. Not…family friends. As people who…"

"Might want to have sex?"

Rachel squeaked, her face getting hot, even though she was alone in her room and no one but her sister had heard that word. "Oh my *God*, Felicity."

"Sorry. It's just that's what moments usually lead to with the Wyatt boys."

"Why? I don't get it. I don't get why we're falling like dominoes for that lot of…"

"Really good guys who also happen to be hot and smart and caring? Who want to protect you, not because they think you're weak or need protecting, but because it's just who they are. On a cellular level."

Rachel expelled a breath. "I don't... I'm twenty-two."

"Is that commentary on the age difference or on being too young to have a serious relationship?"

"Neither. Both. I don't know! Why are we talking about relationships? It was like a moment of... lust. Fleeting lust. Very fleeting."

"Let me tell you this, Rach, lust over a Wyatt is never fleeting. I wasn't exactly planning on doing this whole baby thing yet. But then Gage came along and...boom, lust. And love."

Love. That was *terrifying*. "Just because you four did it, doesn't mean I will."

"Of course it doesn't. You're your own person, and so is Tucker. I'm just trying to say it's normal to be attracted, and to be confused by it since you haven't always had those feelings. Danger and worry has a way of...stripping away our normal walls. When it does that, we can see someone as they actually are instead of how we've always perceived them to be."

"I don't have any walls."

Felicity was quiet for a few seconds. "Okay." She did *not* sound like she agreed. "But Tucker does. Even knowing how awful that childhood before Pauline must have been, I don't think I fully understood it until I saw Gage in that cave with Ace. Knowing Ace would have killed him and felt...justified. It isn't just viciousness and abuse they were raised with, it was...well, insanity."

Felicity paused, and Rachel shuddered. She hated to think about what Gage would have gone through. As a child and as a man. Tucker seemed so…not as afflicted as the others. She knew the older ones had spent longer being at the mercy of Ace Wyatt, but Tucker's eight years were nothing to ignore.

"The point is, being scared churns things up," Felicity continued. "That's okay. It doesn't mean you're weird. It doesn't mean you're not worried about Dad. It just means you're human. And Tucker is hot."

That shocked a laugh out of her. "Aren't you supposed to only have eyes for Gage?"

"Heart and soul for Gage. Eyes for anyone else. Things will be clearer when this is over, and Tucker and the rest of them are working hard to figure out what's going on so Dad can come home."

Rachel wanted to believe her. More than belief, though, she heard something in her sister's voice she wasn't sure she fully ever had before. Felicity had grown up nervous and shy, and she'd slowly come into her own the past few years. But Gage and this pregnancy had really given her an even bigger strength that she'd been afraid to believe in growing up. "You sound happy, Felicity."

"I am. And I'm mad at Dad that he's adding worry to my happy, but that's life. Happy and worry and even attraction can all pile up on each other in the same moment. I'm learning to accept that. I think the the thing is…we were raised right. We've got good instincts. Don't question your instincts."

Rachel let that settle through her. Wasn't that what

she'd been doing? Or maybe she'd been questioning her worth or usefulness but it all kind of added up to the same thing. "Thanks, Felicity. This helped."

"I'm glad. Try to get some rest, Rach."

"You and baby, too."

They said their goodbyes and Rachel climbed into bed. She didn't feel any more clear on the whole Tucker thing, but she felt…more settled.

Don't question your instincts.

She'd be thinking about that a lot over the next few days.

She fell asleep, hopeful for another restful, uninterrupted night. But in the shadows of night came the noise. The rustle. The unearthly glow of cat eyes.

Were they cat eyes? They weren't human but…

Secrets always hurt the innocent. Curtis Washington is going to learn that the hard way.

He had her. He was holding her too tight and she couldn't wiggle away. The eyes weren't his, but they followed. Animal.

The human who had her was someone entirely different. She could hear the hum and scuttle of night life. Could see the moon shining bright from above. But she couldn't see the shadow who carried her too quickly and too easily away from everything she loved.

She squirmed and tried to scream, but she was squeezed too tight—both by the man's grip and her own fear.

When he stopped, it was worse. He wasn't squeezing so tight, but she couldn't breathe at all as he lifted the thing he always lifted, glinting silver in the moonlight. Some kind of…pronged knife. Slashing down at her face.

Run. Wake up.

She always did. Until now.

This time she felt the searing pain of the knife. But a growl, and a thud kept the knife from scoring too deep. It was painful. So painful she thought she might die. She was bleeding and her eyes felt like they were on fire, but the man didn't have her anymore.

TUCKER TOOK THE stairs two at a time, the safety already off on his gun. Rachel's blood-curdling scream had woken him from a fitful sleep, and he'd immediately jumped out of bed and run upstairs.

"Tucker." Sarah stood in the hall in her pajamas, holding a baseball bat.

"Go back to your room," Tucker hissed at her. The screaming had stopped. He inched toward Rachel's room, keeping his footsteps light. He controlled his breathing, pushed all the fear away and focused on the task at hand.

Save her. Now.

He could bust the door open, which was his first instinct. But he didn't know who was behind it, and if he could go for stealthy, he had to. Carefully, he reached out and placed his hand on the door. He willed the slight tremor away with sheer force.

He couldn't afford to be emotional right now. He had a mission. Slowly, carefully, he turned the knob and eased the door open inch by inch.

The room was bathed in light. Rachel sat in the middle of her bed, head in her hands, but Tucker didn't see anyone else.

He immediately swept the room. "Where is he?"

"Tucker." She wrapped the blanket around herself. "What are you doing?"

"I... You screamed." He slowly lowered the gun, belatedly realizing she wasn't in trouble at all. All the fear drained out of him until his knees nearly buckled. "Hell, Rach. That scream could have woken the dead."

"I'm sorry. I'm..." She inhaled shakily and he finally realized she'd been crying. Tears tracked down her cheeks even as she spoke calmly. "I had a bad dream, that's all. I didn't mean to scare you. I..." She shook her head. "Did Sarah wake up?"

"Yeah, but—"

She picked her phone up off the nightstand. "Text Sarah. I'm okay. Bad dream." She dropped her phone, and Sarah burst into the room a few seconds later.

"Oh my God. Rach. How awful. What do you need?"

"Noth—" She seemed to think better of it. "I think I could use a drink."

"I'll be right back." Sarah scurried away.

Tucker studied Rachel. She was shaking, and though she made no noise, fresh tears leaked out of her eyes.

"I'm sorry to have woken you up. I—"

"Stop apologizing," he said, and he knew his voice was too harsh when she winced. But he felt...ripped open. That scream and all the most terrible scenarios that had gone through his mind even as he'd shoved them away to do what needed to be done had taken years off his life.

He let out his own shaky breath. She was okay. Well, not okay. She was crying. Upset. He moved for her bed. "Are they all like this?"

She shook her head, pulling the blanket up to her chin. "No. Usually I wake up before…" She took a steadying breath and he just couldn't take the fear still in her eyes, in her voice. He sat on the very edge of the bed, putting his hand on her shoulder.

She took a deep gulping breath. "It's just I usually wake up before he hurts me. But tonight the knives slashed across my face."

He rubbed his hand up and down her arm. She seemed to need to talk about it, and he had some suspicions now about these dreams. "Knives?"

"A man. He had me. He had this knife or knives with multiple points. He…" She couldn't seem to swallow down a hiccupped sob. She shuddered, so he pulled her closer until she leaned into him.

She let out a little sigh, and some of the shaking subsided. "I could feel it. The pain. The blood. I don't know if it was a memory or made up, but it felt real. And I was small. I had my adult brain, but he could cart me around easily. It was a man, but there was also an animal. I don't think it was a mountain lion. It was more…doglike. And he jumped on the man when he hurt me. That animal saved me, I think."

She shook her head. "It doesn't make sense. I don't

want it to make sense." She buried her head in his shoulder. "I want the dreams to go away and I want Dad to be home."

"Of course you do, sweetheart." He rubbed his hand up and down her back. "So do I." He tried to keep the grimness out of his voice. But this situation was grim. The more she explained the dream, the more he had to wonder if Rachel knew more than she understood.

And he had to wonder if *Duke* knew that. If that was half of why he'd agreed to disappear with North Star on such short notice. To keep Rachel out of it.

"I heard that name again. Curtis Washington. Do you think that's a real person?" She pulled back from him, her gaze meeting his. Her complexion was a little gray, and the faded pink of her scars seemed more pronounced against the brown of her skin. She looked at him earnestly, even though he knew she couldn't see him clearly. "Why am I dreaming this name? I've never thought my dreams were real, but…"

"It keeps repeating. And getting worse."

She nodded. Her face was close to his. Their noses would touch if he leaned just an inch forward. His arm was still around her and she was leaning into him.

In her bed.

Tucker let his arm slip away from her, though he stayed seated at the edge of her bed. He inched even closer to that edge so that, though he was close, their bodies were not in danger of touching, and berated himself for even the second of inappropriate thought that gripped him.

She was shaking, crying and scared.

And very close to a truth he wasn't supposed to let her know about.

"I think we need to look into that name. Don't you? Maybe it has something to do with Dad. Maybe—"

Sarah bustled into the room carrying a tray full of glasses. "I didn't know what kind of drink so I just kind of brought…"

"Everything." Rachel smiled indulgently. "Thank you. I think I'll take the water."

Tucker slid off her bed. He needed to let Sarah take care of this. Comfort her. He needed to escape before she asked him to do what he wasn't supposed to do.

He eyed Sarah's tray, took the shot glass off it and downed the whiskey. He put the glass back, then tried to disappear.

"Tuck, I want to look into the name. I think we have to."

How could he say no to her? "I'll see what I can do."

Chapter Nine

Rachel knew that Tucker would look into the name Curtis Washington, and he was a detective so he'd be able to do far more than her. Still, that didn't mean she couldn't aid him in his search.

If the name connected to everything that was going on, that meant it connected to Dad. And if the dream connected to everything that was going on...

She didn't know what it would mean.

It scared her. That it might be terrible. That it might be buried deep in her subconscious...

"There's a lot of junk up here, Rach. I don't know how we're going to go through it all," Sarah said.

Rachel could tell Sarah was antsy to get outside, to do her work on the ranch, even if it was a rainy, dreary day. But when Rachel had mentioned going up to the attic, Sarah had insisted on helping.

"I know it's overwhelming, but I can't sit around waiting for Tuck to figure it out. I know it was a dream. This is probably insane, but—"

"Look, that's some dream. Maybe normally I'd brush it off, but everything is off right now. Dev is being *nice* to me." The horror in her tone had Rachel smiling.

"That's sweet of him."

"It's creepy as hell." Sarah moved through the attic, and Rachel figured she was doing what she had asked—reading labels of boxes and pulling out anything that seemed relevant. "Speaking of creepy, Tuck was totally checking you out last night."

Rachel nearly stumbled over what she assumed was a box. *"What?"*

"One hundred percent checking out your rack, sis."

Rachel sputtered, and she could feel heat creeping up her face. "Geez, Sarah…"

"I can tell him to knock it off if you want."

"What? No. Oh my God, don't do that!"

"Why not?"

Rachel tried to work through this insane turn in the conversation. "Because that's embarrassing and weird."

"So, not because you'd *like* Tucker to be checking you out. Tucker Wyatt."

"I know who Tucker is," Rachel replied, all too shrilly.

"That doesn't answer my question."

"Did you actually have one?"

"Yeah. Are you creeped out Tuck was looking at your boobs, or do you like it?"

Rachel opened her mouth but no sound came out. She wasn't creeped out, but she wasn't sure if she liked it, either. She was just… "I don't know."

"I mean, in fairness it wasn't like super creeper ogling. It was like…noticing. Your boobs."

"I need this conversation to be over," Rachel muttered. Her face was hot, her heart was hammering and they had way more important concerns at hand. "Whatever we're looking for, it's not going to be in a box. If it's such a secret that Dad had to disappear, it's going to be somewhere…like in the wall. Or out in the stables or something. It'd be hidden."

"But who would go through all this stuff? Wouldn't hiding it in plain sight work just as well?" Sarah asked, thankfully moving away from the subject of Tucker.

"Not if you expected someone to go looking for your secret stuff. If Dad *had* secret stuff—the kind you run away from so your children aren't in the middle of it—it'd be hidden somewhere. Which means there's not going to be a box labeled *secret stuff*. It's going to be harder than that. Sneakier than that."

Sarah blew out a loud breath. "I really hate this."

"Yeah, me, too."

They worked in silence for a while. Sarah went through reading labels on boxes and checking the contents of those unlabeled. Rachel went around the attic perimeter feeling the walls, trying to determine if there was any place that could be hiding something.

She was about to give up when her hands landed on something metal in the corner by the door. It was some kind of box, but instead of cardboard or plastic, it was a heavy metal.

"What's this?"

"Huh." Sarah stepped closer. "It's a locked cashbox type deal, but there's a little piece of masking tape on it that says *buttons*."

"Who would lock up buttons?"

"Mom loved collecting buttons, but I don't think there'd be any reason to lock them up. Here, give it to me."

"If it's locked, how will you—" Rachel began.

There was a squeaking sound and then a crash—like tiny buttons falling across the floor.

"Oops," Sarah said. "Lock was a little easier to break than I thought. But it is just…buttons. Everywhere now. Here, take the box so I can pick up the ones that fell."

Rachel took the box back. She let her fingers trail over the buttons. Mom had loved to collect them. Old grief welled inside of her, though it had been enough years now that she knew how to push it away.

Still, touching something of her mother's had her eyes and nose stinging with unshed tears. She blinked them back as she dug her fingers into the buttons—and touched something with a sharp edge. She cradled the box in her elbow and pulled the item out of the buttons. Using both hands, she felt around the edge of it. Much bigger than a button. Maybe an oddly shaped belt buckle?

"Sarah?"

"Wh— Oh my God."

"What? What is it?"

"It's a police badge." It was snatched out of Rachel's hand. "It says *Officer. Chicago Police.*"

"Chicago? Why would there be a Chicago police badge in a box full of buttons?"

"A *locked* box full of buttons," Sarah pointed out. "If we're looking for secrets, I think we might have found one."

"Are you guys up in the attic?" Tuck's voice called from below.

Rachel felt Sarah press the badge back into her palm. "Your call. You want to hide it, I will. You want to tell him, I'll be right behind you."

"Why are you leaving it up to me? He's your father, too."

"They're your dreams, Rach. And Tucker seems to be your thing. Let's face it, you're the calm, rational one between the two of us. Whatever you want to do is what we should do."

Tucker's form appeared in the doorway. "Hey. Dev's looking for you, Sarah. What are you two doing up here?"

Sarah didn't answer him. Because she'd put it all on Rachel.

"We wanted to poke around and see if we could find something of Dad's. Get some idea of what he might be keeping a secret." She held the badge behind her back, the box of buttons in the crook of her arm. What else might be in there?

And did she want Tuck to know about it?

"I'll go find Dev. See what he wants."

Rachel heard Sarah's retreat as she let her fingers trace the outline of the badge. Chicago Police? Could she picture her father as a police officer?

Or had he had some kind of run in with a police officer? Was this darker? More awful? Should she *want* to hide it from everyone so they never knew?

But how could she bring her father home without help? Without *Tucker's* help. Why wouldn't she trust Tucker Wyatt with everything she found? He was…a Wyatt. He was a good person. He didn't lie. He was a detective who searched for the truth, who's father's sins weighed on him even when they shouldn't.

He was a good man.

Tucker was totally checking you out last night.

"You okay?"

She nodded and cleared her throat. "We found a box of my mom's buttons."

His hand was on her shoulder, giving her a friendly squeeze. "That's a nice thing to have. Even if it makes you sad."

She nodded, because she agreed. Because she knew he didn't have anything from his mother, whatever complicated feelings he might have had about her. And he wouldn't want anything from his father. She had two good, supportive, loving parents who hadn't just loved *her* but had fostered or adopted five other girls over the years and made them all a family.

"I miss her most around this time of year," Tuck said, his voice gentle. "She was always rounding us up, trying to help Grandma Pauline get us ready for school rather than show up the first day looking like feral dogs."

"She used to say you boys needed love, education and a hardheaded woman to keep you on the straight and narrow."

He laughed. "Grandma Pauline did all three. So did your mom."

It was strange to talk to Tucker about her mom. She knew Eva Knight had considered the Wyatt boys part of her own brood. She'd helped Grandma Pauline corral them as much as she could. Mom had loved them. She'd cared about people who needed help, and love, and she'd given hope to those in the darkest places.

Rachel didn't have any dark places. Not really. Even her dreams were just dreams—even if they were pointing to *something*. She wasn't like Liza and Jamison who had survived the Sons, or Felicity who'd survived an abusive father both as a child and then as a woman. She wasn't any of the Wyatt boys with the horror they'd grown up with and escaped.

She'd had a good, mostly easy life. So, Mom had always tasked her with helping, providing for, being the hope.

If there was any hope in this situation with Dad, it was that they could get him home. Secrets wouldn't do that. Being suspicious of Tucker wouldn't do that.

Rachel took a deep breath, feeling around the edge of the badge one more time. Then she held it forward. "I found this in the box of buttons."

TUCKER STARED AT the badge held out in Rachel's hand. Chicago PD. He didn't know how to react. He knew, of course, that it was Duke's, though Rachel probably didn't. Wouldn't.

He wanted to tell her. Not just about her father's past but about everything. North Star and where Duke was.

An equal part of him wanted to laugh it off, stop her from probing into this, from entwining herself in trouble. He wanted to wrap her up in a safe bubble so she didn't have to worry about all this.

But he remembered all too well that terrifying scream that had woken him in the middle of the night. Some of this mystery and danger was inside her subconscious somewhere. No matter what he did—he couldn't protect her from that.

"It's a police badge," he said, his voice a shade too rough.

"Yes. Sarah told me it says *Chicago Police*." She pressed it into his palm. "It has to mean something."

Boy, did it. "Did you check the rest of the box?"

"I haven't had the chance. We'd just found this when you came up."

He frowned over that. "Why didn't Sarah say any-thing?"

"She said she'd give me the choice whether to tell you or not."

"Why wouldn't you tell me?"

Rachel shrugged. "I did tell you, though."

He wasn't sure that was much of a comfort, but he supposed it had nothing to do with the issue at hand. He set the badge aside, then took the box of buttons from her. He found an empty mason jar to dump the buttons into. As he poured them into it, he let the buttons fall over his fingers. There was nothing else big, but as he came to the end of the buttons, a key fell into his fingers.

He held it up, looking at it on both sides. "Nothing else in there except a key."

"A key to what?"

"I don't have a clue. It's just a key."

"It can't *just* be a key."

"Well, no. It was in with the buttons and the badge so it has to be something, but there aren't any hints as to what." Tucker examined the box. It was a rusted out cashbox, nothing special about it. No space for any kind of false bottom.

"A badge and a key. A missing father. Dreams that feel way too close to real." She blew out a breath. "Anything else life wants to throw at me?"

"Please don't go taunting the universe like that."

Her mouth curved. "You don't honestly believe in curses and jinxes?"

"*Believe* might be a strong word. Let's say I have a healthy respect for the possibility."

Rachel shook her head, though she was still smiling. A beam of sunlight shone in front of her, making dust motes dance around her face. He'd always *known* she was pretty, but something about doing all this made him *feel* it.

Maybe he wholeheartedly believed in curses and

jinxes, because his sudden attraction for Rachel felt like both.

She frowned. "Did you hear that?"

He hadn't heard much of anything except his own stupidity. "What?"

"I'm not sure. Like an engine, but…" She trailed off and he strained to hear what she heard. Everything was silent, but he felt the need to hold himself still, and continue to strain to hear long after the moment had passed.

Creak.

Rachel's frown deepened, and she opened her mouth, presumably to say something, but Tucker laid his hand gently over her mouth.

She'd heard an engine. He'd heard the creak of a floorboard under the weight of someone. If it was any Wyatt or Knight, they would have announced themselves—or they'd know which boards to avoid.

Tucker scanned the attic. Maneuvering Rachel to hide her would make noise. Everything would make noise, and whoever or whatever had creaked the floorboard had gone silent again. He was too far from the tiny window letting in the light to see through it and scan the surroundings.

He didn't wear his gun around the house because he was afraid it would make Sarah and Rachel nervous, and now he mentally kicked himself for caring more about feelings than safety.

He'd have to fight off whoever was at that door. He'd need the element of surprise. And to do it all while keeping Rachel out of the way.

There was only one way to do it, since once the attic door opened it would open this way and give whoever was on the stairs clear sight of Rachel.

But if he hid on the other side of the door, he could come at whoever it was from behind. They might know he was up here, but Rachel would be a momentary distraction he'd use.

He pressed his mouth as close to her ear as he could. Spoke as softly as humanly possible. "You're going to stay right here. Don't move unless I tell you to. Squeeze my hand if you understand."

When she squeezed, he squeezed right back. He was loathe to let go of her, to do what he knew he needed to do. He wanted to promise her things would be okay. He wanted to be a human shield between her and hurt.

But he had to stop doing what was most comfortable, and start doing what was the safest. He moved in absolute silence to the opposite side of the door.

He waited, counting his heartbeats, keeping his breathing even. Rachel's life rested in his hands, so he could not focus on panic or worry or that heavy responsibility. He could only focus on eradicating the threat.

The door squeaked, the narrow opening slowly growing. He saw the barrel of a gun first. It was pointed down at the ground, but he couldn't take any chances.

He waited until he actually saw an arm, then pushed the door as hard as he could. The gun didn't clatter to the ground as he'd hoped, but the intruder had stumbled back onto the stair.

"Get down, Rach," he commanded, moving through the door and closing it behind him. A figure in all black was on the stairs. The figure didn't raise the gun, but that didn't mean it wasn't dangerous.

The figure struck out, and Tucker managed to block most of the blow. They grappled, exchanging punches and elbows and kicks. Eventually they both stumbled, crashing down the first flight of stairs and onto the landing that would go down to the second floor.

Tucker banged up his elbow pretty good, and he'd landed on the side with his phone in his pocket so not only did a shooting pain go through his hip, but he was pretty sure the phone was crushed.

He swore, and so did the figure. Tuck frowned. It was a woman. He noticed blond hair had escaped the black ski mask she wore. He scrambled to his feet, recognizing her as the woman who'd first approached him on behalf of North Star, then again outside his office.

"You." Why was the woman from North Star sneaking through the house? Pointing a gun and fighting with him?

The woman glared up at him, then landed a kick to his stomach, and he cursed himself for being caught off guard. She made a run for it to go up the stairs, but Tucker got his breath back quickly enough to grab her by the foot. He heard her let out a curse as she crashed into the stairs.

"Why are Wyatts always ruining my life?" she demanded, kicking back at him.

"What the hell are you doing? North Star is supposed to be the good guys."

She stopped kicking and fighting him off and gave a derisive snort before rolling onto her back. Tucker had the sense she could easily kick him down the stairs and there wouldn't be much he could do about it.

"I have my orders, from those *good* guys." The woman jerked her chin toward the attic "She knows something. She needs to come with me or our mission is compromised. Granger knew you'd be difficult about it."

"How do you know she knows something?" Tucker demanded. How on earth could they know about Rachel's dreams?

The woman gave him a withering glare. "We know everything, Wyatt. Haven't you caught on?"

It didn't matter. It couldn't. "Screw your mission. She's got nothing to do with it and you know it. You're going to drag an innocent into the midst of this? Via kidnapping?"

The woman's expression went grim, but Tucker thought he saw a flash of conscience. "I have my orders," she repeated.

Which told Tucker she didn't particularly want to follow those orders.

"Excuse me?" Both he and the woman he'd fought looked up at the top of the stairs. Rachel stood with her arms over her chest, expression furious. "Maybe one of you could tell me what's going on and I, the woman in question, can decide for myself?"

Chapter Ten

Rachel was shaking, but she'd wrapped her arms around herself to keep it from showing. She was at the top of the stairs and from what she could tell, Tucker and…some woman he knew were on the landing in the middle of the stairs having an argument about her.

"Rach."

"No, I don't think I want you to tell me," she said, holding on to her composure by a very thin thread. Tucker had been lying to her, that much was clear.

"Listen. My name is Shay. I'm with the North Star Group. Tucker and Cody Wyatt have worked for us. Your father's past connected to ours, so we're helping him out. If you come with me—"

"What a load of bull. You're not helping him. You're using him," Tucker said disgustedly. "If you're taking her against her will, you're not in this to protect anyone."

"No one said it was against my will, Tucker."

She heard him take a few stairs. "She was damn

well going to, Rachel. She snuck in here, and she fought me—"

"You started that," Shay interrupted.

"She was going to kidnap you. Because you know things about your father's past. Not because she wants to protect you or Duke, but because they'll do anything to bring down the Sons. Including letting innocent people get hurt."

There was a heavy, poignant silence.

"Don't have anything to say to that?" Tucker said scathingly to the woman.

Who still didn't say anything. Rachel didn't understand any of this, but she understood one thing. "You have my father."

"We're helping your father," this Shay person said. "It's what we do."

"What does this have to do with the Sons?" she asked. Because of course it did. Tucker had lied to her and her father was in danger because of the Sons of the Badlands.

What else was new?

"Rachel, listen to me—"

"You knew where he was, who he was being protected by and *why*, but you didn't think to share that with me?" Her throat closed with every word, until the last one was a squeak.

"Rach." He sounded pained, hurt.

But she couldn't have any sympathy for him. He'd lied to her. Let her worry and fear and… He'd used her. Even if he was right about this North Star Group using Dad instead of helping him, Tucker had used her. Knowing…everything.

"If I go with you, what happens?" she said, addressing Shay.

"I'd take you to your father."

"Oh, that's low," Tucker said sourly. "She would not. They would interrogate you about your dreams until they got the information they wanted. If you give them what they want, they *might* let you see Duke, but considering they're using him as bait, I don't think that's happening anytime soon. They need him. They need the information they think you might have. What they don't need is a father–daughter reunion. And who knows, they might use you as bait, too. You can't go with her, Rachel."

"She's coming with me. Whether she does it willingly or not, my mission is to bring her back. So I will."

But Rachel noted they were standing in the attic staircase having this conversation. Shay wasn't making a move to fight Tucker anymore. She hadn't yet attempted to take Rachel against her will like she was saying she would.

"Can you promise my father will be okay if I go with you willingly?"

There was a hesitation. "I…can't promise that. Your father's in a dangerous situation."

"Think, Rachel," Tuck implored her. "I know you're mad at me. Maybe you'll never forgive me. I get it. But think about your father. What would he want you to do?"

"I don't care as much about what he'd want me to do as what I can do to protect him."

"They'd use whatever you gave them to complete their mission. You and Duke would be collateral damage." Tucker sounded so…desperate. So intent. It wasn't his usual self.

But his usual self had been lying to her. Should she have seen it? There had been hints. Hesitations. A carefulness.

The woman was suspiciously silent at Tucker's accusation. "Is that true?" Rachel asked quietly.

There was a long silence. "It's not…untrue."

"So, you're both liars who don't care about anyone?"

"Your father wanted you safe," Tucker said, and while he was being contrite, so to speak, there was a thread of steel in his words. "You and Sarah. Why do you think I'm here? He—"

"You saw him. Before he disappeared. You saw him and you lied to all of us."

She couldn't see his expression, but she knew all those accusations landed like blows. Unless he was a completely different man than she'd always believed. Which maybe he was.

"He wanted you and Sarah protected," Tucker repeated, and his voice was rough. She wanted to believe that was emotion. Guilt.

She just didn't know what to believe about him anymore. He'd seen her father. He'd let her worry.

He'd comforted her after her dreams. Stepped in and made meals, cleaned up. He'd taught her self-defense and…maybe he'd tried to ease some of her fears. She thought of the badge, the key.

"Were you lying about looking into the name?"

Tucker was silent for ticking awful seconds where she wanted to curl into herself and cry. Just…disappear from this world where the man she trusted was such a liar.

"I wasn't lying. I looked into it. I was told to leave it be."

"In fairness, he didn't leave it be," Shay said. "Which is why I'm here."

"You guys are keeping some kind of tabs on me?" Tucker growled as if he was both surprised and disgusted by the information. "What the hell is this?"

"It's business, Wyatt. The business of taking down the Sons."

"I'm so tired of people trying to take down the Sons," Rachel said, her voice growing louder with every word. "I'm so tired of people getting hurt because of the *Sons*. My father and I have nothing to do with them. Why can't you leave us alone?"

"Listen, you can dismiss me and all, but neither of you actually have a say. If I don't take you, they'll send someone else. You're a part of North Star's mission now. They won't just take no for an answer. It'd be easier if you just came with me."

Rachel didn't know why that was the straw that broke the camel's back. "And I am really done doing what's *easier* for everyone else."

Tucker had to ignore the searing pain in his chest. The slick black weight of guilt. He had to focus on

getting Rachel out of this mess. Once she was safe…
Well, he could self-flagellate and she could hate him
forever.

He rubbed at his chest.

"If you don't come with me of your own volition,"
Shay said in a careful, emotionless voice, "I'll take
you by force."

Tucker had already positioned himself between
Shay and Rachel. He was ready to fight. He didn't
think Shay would use the gun against him. At least
he hoped not.

"She is an innocent bystander. Whatever she
knows is wrapped up in nightmares she can't un-
tangle." He thought about the badge, the key he'd
slid into his pocket. He could give that to Shay as a
peace offering. It might even help Duke, and it wasn't
that he thought North Star was evil—they just didn't
care about people. They cared about their mission.

As for him, he cared about too many people involved to let this go so far as to touch Rachel. The
key might be some kind of insurance if he kept it.
So, he had to.

Tucker turned to Rachel. She held herself impos-
sibly still, her expression mostly blank. Except her
eyes. They were hurt. Betrayed.

And he'd done the betraying.

He had to get her out of this. Maybe she'd never
forgive him, but if he could get her out of this, maybe
he could forgive himself.

"Your father wanted me to protect you from this.
Keep you separate."

"But I'm *not* separate. If they're here about my dreams, there's something real in them." Her eyebrows drew together. "It has to be real."

"That doesn't mean you have to put yourself in danger. It doesn't mean you have to go with this group who doesn't care about you."

"This group has my father."

"You going there doesn't help him. It helps *them*." He wouldn't let her go. Even if she wanted to. But maybe he could assuage at least some of his guilt if she'd just understand the truth here. A truth he hadn't fully understood until now.

Maybe North Star wanted to take down the Sons, but they didn't care enough about the innocent collateral damage involved.

"Oh, just someone punch me," Shay said with no small amount of exasperation.

"What?" Tucker demanded, turning from Rachel to face her.

"In the face." She pointed to her nose. "Make it good, too."

"What are you talking about?"

"I can't go back to Granger unscathed *and* with you having gotten away. You need to make it look like you beat me. Literally and figuratively."

Finally, what Shay was saying got through. She was…letting them go. "I… I can't punch a woman."

She rolled her eyes. "I can punch you first if it gets you going."

"That's not—"

"I'll do it," Rachel said, walking down the stairs. She stopped on the stair right above Shay.

"No offense, but—"

Rachel squared like he'd taught her, curled her fist and landed a blow right to Shay's face.

Swearing in time with Rachel, Shay gingerly placed her palm on her jaw, working it back and forth. Rachel shook out her hand, then cradled it.

"Well, that'll work," Shay said. "Hell."

"You really think one punch is going to convince them?"

"I can handle the rest, but I couldn't punch my own self in the face." She gave Rachel a once-over. "Not half bad. Keep working on that and you might be one hell of a fighter." She moved as if to leave, but Tucker stepped in front of her on the stairs.

"I should take your gun."

She grimaced, clearly loathing the idea of losing her weapon.

"They can't think you got back in one piece still armed, can they?"

"Yeah, yeah, yeah." She handed over the weapon.

Still, Tucker couldn't move out of her way. "Will they kick you out?"

She shrugged. "Not if I quit first."

"Why would you do that?"

"Because you're right, Wyatt. I'm not in the business of hurting innocent people for the sake of a mission. North Star didn't start out that way, but lately… Doesn't matter. It's getting old and maybe this is my last straw. You're going to need to run, though. Whether I get kicked out or quit—they'll keep coming for her. She knows stuff." Shay let out a sigh. "That phone Granger gave you?"

Tucker pulled it out of his pocket. It was in a couple pieces after his fall down the stairs.

Shay nodded. "That's good. Leave it here."

It dawned on Tucker that meant Granger had been tracking him, maybe listening to him. He'd know about everything up to the fight on the stairs. He nodded grimly at Shay, tossing the phone onto the ground. He smashed it once more under his heel for good measure.

Shay looked back at Rachel, then leaned close to whisper to Tucker. "Get her out of here ASAP. Whatever she knows, they'll use it. Not to help or protect Knight, but to get the Sons. I want the Sons destroyed as much as anybody, and I imagine you do, too, but good people shouldn't be used as bait to take them down."

"If you don't quit, if you don't get kicked out, you could help keep Duke safe. From the inside."

She smiled wryly. "That's a lot of ifs."

"Like you said, we both want to bring down the Sons. We just don't want innocent people hurt in the process. We could work together on this."

She shook her head. "You and your brother. Two peas in a dumb, naive pod."

"Is that a yes?"

She blew out a breath. "Look, I'll do what I can. That does *not* mean we're working together. Be clear on that."

He wasn't sure he believed her, and when he held out a hand for a shake, she shook her head. "We are *not* partners. Be best for you both if you get out of here before I do."

Tucker nodded and looked up at Rachel. Her expression was grim. But Shay was right, they had to get out of here. He didn't know where yet, but he'd figure it out.

What he wasn't so sure he was going to figure out was how to live with what he'd done.

Chapter Eleven

Tucker stole a horse.

Maybe it was harsh for Rachel to consider it stealing, considering it was *her* horse, and she was one of the people riding it, but it felt like stealing. It felt like lying and scaring the people she loved by disappearing.

Like Dad did?

She didn't even have time to wallow in the betrayal of it all because Shay was absolutely telling the truth, no doubt about it. Someone else would come for her, because her dreams were true.

True.

They rode Buttercup away from the ranch—in the opposite direction of the pasture Dev and Sarah were working in this afternoon. It felt really stupid to be riding a horse named Buttercup when trying to escape a group that was trying to bring down the Sons—which was what she wanted.

How could two groups of people want the same thing and disagree so fundamentally on how to get there?

She didn't speak as Tucker explained everything from the beginning. His helping out North Star. Being ready to quit before he walked into a diner with the North Star guy and her father.

Her father. Who'd brought down dirty cops as a young man and was somehow paying for it over thirty years later.

Her father wasn't who she'd thought. Tucker wasn't who she'd thought.

Oh, that probably wasn't fair. In fact, it was really quite *Wyatt* of Tucker to want to save the day without telling her. Still, no matter how justified, the fact he'd lied to her and she'd bought it hook, line and sinker… It hurt.

Maybe his deception was necessary, but how easily he'd fooled her made her feel stupid. And weak. Now she was riding a horse, with Tucker's hard body directly behind her, through the rolling hills of southeastern South Dakota like she was some kidnapped bride on the prairie.

Rachel didn't say anything as they rode, and after he'd told the whole story, neither did Tucker. She didn't know how many hours they rode in silence, how many miles they covered. She didn't know where they were going and she didn't ask.

Because she was too afraid he'd offer another lie, and she'd believe it as gospel.

"Sun's going down," Tucker said, his voice rusty with disuse. "We should camp."

"Camp," Rachel echoed. Up to this point, she hadn't been afraid, not really. In the moments Tucker had been fighting Shay, yes, but after that there'd been too many other feelings. Sadness, fury, hurt and the ache in her hand from punching Shay had taken up too much space to be truly afraid.

But now the idea of camping had those beats of panic starting in her chest.

"I'm sorry. It's the only way," Tucker said gently. He brought the horse to a halt and he got off. Since she couldn't see the ground, she had to let him help her dismount.

Rachel immediately pulled away from his grasp, though she kept her feet in the same place since she couldn't be sure she wouldn't trip and fall.

"So, what's the plan?" she asked flatly.

He handed her something. Her cane. It took her a moment to register that and to take it. They'd left in such a hurry, but he'd thought to grab her probing cane.

After lying to you about everything.

"Right now? The plan is to keep you away from North Star."

"For how long?" she asked.

"As long as we need to."

"We're just going to camp in the hills until someone magically alerts us to the fact North Star no longer needs me?"

"You still have your phone," he reminded her.

"It doesn't have service out here." She was completely alone in the wilderness with a man who…who she'd trusted and who'd lied to her. About the most important things. "Sarah is going to be worried sick."

"She would be worried sick if you'd stayed—because Shay would have taken you, or someone else would have come and finished the job. At least she'll know you're with me."

It was true, but that didn't make it comforting. Maybe because she knew Tucker would have stood up for her. He would have fought and protected her against all the people North Star sent. Liar that he was. "I don't camp."

"I know," he said, with enough weight that she figured he understood it was because it reminded her of that night. Of her memories or dreams. She'd been alone in the wilderness when the mountain lion had attacked, or at least that's what she'd believed until lately.

"I'm sorry this has touched you, Rachel. I wish I could make it not."

She wanted to ask him if that was another lie, but she understood in that statement that while Tucker had lied to her about facts, he'd never lied to her about feelings. He'd promised to try to keep her father safe—and he had been working to do that. He'd promised her father to keep her out of it.

He'd failed, and likely was busy heaping all sorts of guilt on himself. She wished that made her feel better, but it actually deflated some of her anger.

"He's my father. It was always going to touch me no matter what you did, Tucker."

He didn't respond, and she could hear the sounds of him making camp. He'd gotten her out of the

One Minute" Survey

You get up to **FOUR books**
<u>and</u> TWO Mystery Gifts...

See inside for details.

Dear Reader,

Your opinions are important to us. So if you'll participate in our fa
and free "One Minute" Survey, **YOU** can pick up to four wonderf
books that **WE** pay for!

As a leading publisher of women's fiction, we'd love to hear from
you. That's why we promise to reward you for completing our
survey.

IMPORTANT: Please complete the survey and return it. We'll ser
your Free Books and Free Mystery Gifts right away. **And we pay
for shipping and handling too!** *We pay for EVERYTHING!*

Try **Harlequin® Romantic Suspense** books featuring heart-racing
page-turners with unexpected plot twists and irresistible chemis
that will keep you guessing to the very end.

Try **Harlequin Intrigue® Larger-Print** books featuring action-pack
stories that will keep you on the edge of your seat. Solve the crir
and deliver justice at all costs.

Or TRY BOTH!

Thank you again for participating in our "One Minute"
Survey. It really takes just a minute (or less) to complete the
survey… and your free books and gifts will be well worth it!

Sincerely,

Pam Powers

Pam Powers
for Reader Service

"One Minute" Survey

GET YOUR FREE BOOKS AND FREE GIFTS!

✓ Complete this Survey   ✓ Return this survey

READER SERVICE—Here's how it works:

house so quickly she didn't know how he'd had time to gather supplies, but he seemed to have enough.

"I know you don't want to camp. I wish there was another way," he finally said, so grave and... It wasn't fair. She couldn't be mad at him when he was beating himself up.

"You know, the same thing would have happened even if you'd told us the truth from the beginning. Didn't Shay basically say that phone North Star gave you was tracking everything?"

"Maybe if I'd been a better liar, you'd be just fine at home."

"Is that what you want? To be a better liar?"

He expelled a loud breath. "No."

"That's why you were going to quit. Well, Dad threw a wrench in your plans, and so did my dreams."

"That sounds a lot like absolution. And misplaced blame."

"It's neither. You did what you had to do. And I can't control my dreams."

"You should be mad at me."

"Oh, I am," she told him. "I'm mad at you. I'm irritated with myself. I'm downright furious with Dad. I don't want to camp. I don't want to run. I don't want any of this."

"I'm sor—"

"I don't want your apologies, either. I want the lies to end. And I want Dad back in one piece. So, we have to figure out how we're going to do that. We can't wait. We can't play the hide-Rachel-away-in-a-safe-corner game. We have to fight. For my father. We have to help him. However we can."

RACHEL SOUNDED FIERCE, and looked it, standing there in the fading daylight, probing cane grasped in one hand, the other clenched in a fist. Her expression was hard and determined.

He wished he could agree. Immediately support her. "If I knew how to do that, I would have already done it."

It was humbling to admit. He'd seen no real way to help Duke except protect Rachel and he'd failed. He'd brought her more into the fold by not suspecting McMillan might be listening in.

The bastard had listened in on private conversations. Rachel's dream aftermath. Talking about her mother and the buttons.

He fingered the key in his pocket. Duke already knew his past. There were no secrets to be uncovered. Whatever the key unlocked, Duke knew about it. Had locked something up. It wouldn't help him now. In fact, it was probably best if it stayed buried.

"Dad's being threatened by this Vianni family, through the Sons, according to North Star."

"It's not just North Star's story. Your father was there when McMillan told me about it. It's true."

She nodded sharply. "Okay. It's true. North Star is supposed to keep him safe, but both you and Shay acted like they're trying to use Dad as some kind of bait to get enough evidence on the Sons. But to what end? To arrest them all? Kill them all?"

"I'm not privy to North Star's plans."

"No, but Shay said that it's gotten too mission focused. They're not caring about people. I don't want Dad to be collateral damage."

"I don't either, Rachel."

"I know you don't." She moved forward using her cane to avoid the dips and bumps in the ground.

Tucker had found the flattest, most even ground he could, but he'd wanted to stay in the hills and trees as much as possible.

"But North Star knows everything about Dad, and presumably they know a lot about the Viannis and the Sons. They don't *need* him there."

"They're protecting him."

"Are they?" she returned. "Or did they say that to you, maybe even to him, but what they really meant is they're using him?"

It was a horrible thought. Even if he didn't agree with everything North Star had done, he believed in their mission. "Your Dad went to them willingly. He had some connection to their leader. Or the leader's dad. Something about him being the reason he had this WITSEC life here. He had to believe they were going to…fix things or he wouldn't have gone."

"But I don't. I don't believe that at all. When one of their own, a woman sent to take me, let's us go instead… Something is very, very wrong. I want my father out. Screw their mission. *You* said that."

"I did. And I meant it in regard to Shay's particular mission of kidnapping you. But I don't want to sabotage North Star. Even if I don't approve of their methods, I approve of what they're doing. I *support* what they're doing." How had this gotten so messed up? "Bringing down the Sons is important."

"It is. Should my father die for it?"

"I don't think North Star would let that happen." But their attempted kidnapping of Rachel made him uncomfortably concerned.

"You don't *think*."

Tucker raked his hands through his hair. "People are after him. Dangerous people. Regardless of the Sons or North Star, your father was a target."

"Because he did something right. Don't you know what that's like?"

It snapped something in him. That leash on his temper and his emotions he fought so hard to keep tethered. "Yeah, I do. I know it's living your life in fear, wondering when it shows up to take you down. I know it's watching your brothers get hurt over and over again by this thing you escaped, while you can't do a damn thing about it. Knowing you don't even rate to be a target because apparently you're not that much of a threat to their kind of evil. I know what it's all like, Rachel, and I'm telling you, *we* can't do anything about it."

She blinked. "Tuck—"

He was so horrified by his torrent of words that had nothing to do with her or this situation, he turned his back on her. "No. It's not about me. It's about Duke."

"Tucker—"

"I said no. I won't steal your father out of the

North Star's hands, not with you. I can't protect you both from all the different forces after you. I got you out of there so they can't use you, can't use your dreams. Because Duke would have wanted me to keep you safe and because it's the right thing." Because the thought of putting her in any more danger just about ripped him in two.

He had to stop this…*emotion*. It was weak. It was…

Wasn't that what Ace told you? Emotion is weak? Caring is weak?

"Would you do it without me?" Rachel asked firmly, breaking through those old memories of his father.

He'd promised to not let himself lose control. The whole tirade about the Sons and his brothers was bad enough. He wouldn't say anything else stupid. But how could she say that? How could she think he'd leave her behind? To think he'd ever, *ever* let her be a target.

He moved to her, telling himself to keep it locked down. He didn't lose his temper. He didn't lose control. Not because emotions were weak as Ace had always said, but because he had to handle this.

But he wanted to grab her by the arms and shake her. He wanted to do all manner of impossible, disastrously ill-advised things.

Instead, he stood in front of her, maybe a few inches too close, and kept his voice ruthlessly controlled. "Let's make one thing very, very clear. There is not a damn thing I will do without you right now."

She stood very still. The sun had disappeared behind the hills, though there was enough light to still make her out. She wouldn't be able to see anything, even shapes in this light. Still, she moved unerringly into him, wrapping her arms around him.

A hug. A comfort.

He couldn't return it. He couldn't push her away. He could only stand there still as a statue, her arms around him and her cheek pressed to his chest.

"Hell, Rach. Be mad at me. Hate me. I can't stand you being nice to me right now."

"I guess it's too bad for you, because I can't stand to be mad at you right now." She pulled back, tilted her head up toward his. "If you told me right now, promised me right now, that you won't lie again, I'll believe you."

Even knowing he shouldn't, he placed his palm on her cheek. "I'm sorry. I can't do that."

Chapter Twelve

Rachel didn't move away from his hand, even though Tucker's words were…not what she'd expected. At all. She liked the warmth of his calloused palm on her cheek, and she liked how close he was as night descended around them.

She shouldn't be concerning herself with warmth. Or how nice it felt. When he was telling her that he wouldn't promise not to lie.

"Why not?" she asked, and the fact it came out a breathy whisper surprised her, as much as the fact he didn't remove his hand. Instead, his thumb brushed back and forth over her cheekbone.

A sparkling heat shimmered underneath her skin, in her blood. She didn't understand it. Not when it was Tucker touching her, but she could hardly deny it existed. The feeling was too big and real and potent.

His voice was low and rough when he spoke. "I can't promise to never lie. I lied to Brady and Cecilia last month. It was one of the hardest things I've ever done—to lie to my brother like that. Knowing they were both suspicious of me. But I'd do it all over again. I'd have to. Because I was trying to accomplish something good and right. If I had to lie to protect you, Rachel, I would. Any of you. Your sisters. My brothers. Your father. Anyone."

She might not have believed him, except she knew from Cecilia he had definitely lied to Brady. His own brother. Even when Cecilia had been convinced he'd been turned into a Sons member, Brady had trusted him. Even with the lies.

If his own brother could—did—how could she not?

"Okay." She didn't dare nod because he might take his hand away. "Okay."

"We'll camp tonight, and maybe in the morning we'll have a clearer idea of what to do. I managed to grab enough supplies for a day or two for us and Buttercup. This is temporary. Until we figure out how to fix this."

She had no idea how they were going to do that, but it didn't feel so impossible with Tucker touching her. Despite everything, she believed in him. He'd gotten them this far. He'd fought off Shay. Convinced her to let them go.

"I want my dad to be safe. I don't want this awful thing to come back and hurt him. He did the right thing, and he had to give up his whole life. It isn't right that he managed to build a new one and they want to take it away from him."

"No, it isn't. If I knew what to do… If I had any clue, I'd do it. *That* I can promise you."

She nodded, the scrape of his rough hand against her cheek a lovely, sparkling distraction from the fear and confusion roiling inside of her.

He didn't need to promise her anything, but of course he would. She had a plethora of *good* men in her life, and it often insulated her to the fact that bad people like Ace Wyatt and whoever was after her father existed. She so seldom remembered what an enormous miracle it was that Tucker and his brothers had escaped the Sons and become...them.

Good men, determined to do good in the world. Maybe not perfectly. He had his issues. That whole spiel about not being worth the Sons' notice because he wasn't a threat.

If anything underscored all her hurt, it was *that*. Tucker put on a face for the world that he was perfectly adjusted, a good detective, brother, man. And he was those things.

But he didn't think he was.

She didn't know how to make him believe he was all the things *she* thought he was. She could only lean into his hand, lean into *him* and this feeling.

She still didn't know how she felt about being attracted to Tucker, about the possibility he felt the same way. She didn't want to be a domino of Knight girls falling in a line for the Wyatt boys.

But everything swirled inside of her obscuring what she didn't want. She could only think of what she did.

"If they don't think you're a threat, they don't understand you. Caring about people isn't a weakness, Tucker." She placed her hand on his chest when the moment didn't evaporate like she'd been afraid it would. "You don't need to be in North Star or putting yourself in mortal danger to be as strong as your brothers, as important. You solve problems. You take *care* of people. That's just as important as putting your life on the line."

He inhaled sharply, but his hand was still on her face. He was so close, their bodies brushing in the increasing darkness around them. "Rach, I don't know what to say to all that."

His voice was as rough as his hand. He was as strong as she'd said, standing there so close. She couldn't resist tipping her mouth up…wishing for something she'd promised herself she couldn't possibly want.

Then his mouth touched hers. Featherlight. No one had ever kissed her before, and she'd always figured it would take some miracle—getting off the ranch, away from her overprotective father and sisters, into a life that was independent and hers, and when would *that* ever happen.

But it was Tucker Wyatt. She didn't need to convince him she was independent—even when he was protecting her, it was only because that's what he *did*.

It ended far too quickly. The kiss. His hand on her cheek. The sound his footsteps made had her thinking he stumbled back and away, as if he'd realized whom he'd kissed.

"We should get some sleep," he said, his voice tight.

She barked out a laugh, couldn't seem to help the reaction. He'd *kissed* her and he was talking about going to sleep. He was ignoring it. Coward. "You kissed me."

"Forget it. It was… Just forget that."

"Forget it? Why would I?"

"Wrong place. Wrong time. Wrong everything."

She frowned at that. Intellectually, he was probably right. Wrong time certainly, which went along with place. But… "It didn't feel so wrong."

"Well, it was," he said firmly.

So firmly that she thought maybe she was missing something. "Why?"

"*Why?* Because…"

She waited impatiently for him to come up with this reason she was missing. "Because?" she demanded when he was just silent.

"Because you're…you're like a sister to me."

She snorted. It was such a pathetic grasping at straws. "Then you're a pervert, Tucker. You don't check out your sister's boobs and then kiss her."

"I didn't! I never…"

"Sarah said you did."

"I…"

"Maybe you can't promise to lie to me, but if you lie to me about *this*, I won't forgive you. Period."

He was quiet for a long stretched-out moment. "I don't know what you want me to say."

"Why did you kiss me?"

"You want the truth? Here and now of all places? Fine. Maybe I owe that to you after all this. Yeah, I'm attracted to you. I don't have a clue as to why… why *now*. I just am. It's just there. Then you had to go say all that stuff, looking up at me like you meant it."

"I can't see," she pointed out, hoping to lighten the moment.

"You know what I mean," he replied gruffly.

"Yeah, I think I do." Unfortunately that made her all the more gooey-hearted when they had much more important things to deal with. Still, truth for truth was only fair. "I meant it, Tuck. I did. And I… guess I'm attracted to you, too."

"You guess," he muttered disgustedly.

Which almost made her smile. "I'm still working through all that. I haven't exactly had a lot of experience with this."

He groaned. "Please God, tell me that wasn't your first kiss."

"Okay, I won't tell you."

He swore a few times, and she had no idea why that made her want to laugh.

"Look. We need to…go to sleep. Tomorrow, we'll come up with a plan. No more of…this stuff."

"This *stuff*?"

"Whatever this is, we'll figure it out when we're not camping in the South Dakota wilderness, with absolutely no plan on how we're going to accomplish what we want. For now, we get some rest and focus on the important things."

She nodded as though she agreed with him, and let him lead her into the tent.

TUCKER WOKE UP in his own personal nightmare. He had to come up with a plan to save Duke, to keep Rachel safe. To outwit North Star, the Sons and some other group of people out for blood.

All knowing he'd kissed Rachel. And now she was

curled up next to him. Because he'd only had time to grab the pack out of his truck—which was outfitted for one person. A tiny tent and *one* sleeping bag.

It was edging far enough into fall that nights were cold, so he'd had to let her cozy up next to him and fall asleep. All while pretending that kiss had never happened.

It was the only way to survive this. Put a brick wall around his own personal slip-up. Seal it off and forget it.

But he'd never in a million years be able to forget the feel of his lips on hers. Simple kisses weren't supposed to…do that. Make you forget who you were and what was important: safety. Hers most of all.

But he'd forgotten everything except her for those humming seconds—not just the kiss, but her talking to him like she understood him. When it felt like no one did.

He knew his brothers saw him as an equal. They couldn't understand that he didn't *feel* like one.

Right now in this warm tent, Rachel's hair curling against his cheek, the soft rise and fall of her chest matching time with his… Well, he supposed Rachel seeing through his issues was a better line of thought than how good she felt here against him.

She shifted, yawned, her eyes slowly blinking open. Even though she wouldn't be able to see in the dim light of the tent, he could see. The sleep slowly lift. Realization and understanding dawning.

And the way she definitely did not try to slide

away or disengage from him, but seemed perfectly content to cuddle closer.

There was a very large part of him that wanted to test it out, too. To see what it would be like to relax into her. To touch her face again. To recognize the soft curves of her body as they pressed to his. To kiss her and—

No. Not possible.

Carefully, he disengaged from her arms and scooted away from her as best he could in the tiny tent.

"Maybe we should go back. I've got nothing. My brothers might have some ideas. They're better at this than I am."

She was quiet for a while as she pushed herself up into a sitting position. "Are they better at it, or were they just put in a position you weren't?"

"You don't need to keep defending me. I don't have low self-esteem. I—"

"You've got issues, Tuck. Good news is, we all do. Better news, you have someone around who's not going to let you believe the crap you tell yourself. So…" She yawned. "I don't suppose you have any coffee?"

He didn't know how to stay in this tiny tent with her looking sleepy and rumpled and gorgeous, talking about how everyone had issues. "I've got some instant. I'll go warm up some water." He didn't *dive* for the tent opening, but he got outside in record time.

The sun was just beginning to rise and the grass held the tiniest hint of frost. It was cold, made colder by the fact that the tent had been so warm. He shivered against the chill as he zipped the tent back up.

A piece of paper fluttered to the ground next to him. Tuck whirled around, scanning the area. But there was nothing except the soft whisper of the wind against the rolling hills of ranch land.

He crouched down, studied the note on the grass. It was wet from the dew, and all he could figure was that it had been left on the tent, and opening the flap had knocked it off.

He looked around, scanning all he could see for any sign of human life or movement. But the world was quiet, with only the interruption of birdsong.

He picked the paper up and opened the fold. Water had smudged the first word, but Tucker could figure it out and read the rest clearly.

Rachel knows the key and the lock.

Tucker flipped the paper over. Nothing on the back. Nothing else on the front. Just one sentence. That didn't make any sense.

The key and the lock? He thought of the key in his pocket. But what did it unlock? And Rachel definitely didn't act like she had any idea what the key was to.

"Rach." He unzipped the flap again and stuck his head in. She was crouched over, rolling up the sleeping bag. He could tell she'd already tidied what few things were inside. "I found something."

She yawned again. "I take it not coffee." She sighed. "What is it?"

"A note. I… I think this is Duke's handwriting."

He frowned, studied it. He wasn't a handwriting expert, and he'd never spent much time scrutinizing Duke's writing, but it certainly looked like his typical slanted scratch.

Tuck looked around the campsite again. He hadn't heard anyone so it was near impossible Duke had left the note for them. He was a big man, and even if he'd been a cop in a former life, stealth was not Duke's current skill. "It was on the tent, then when I opened the flap it fell to the ground."

The only one who knew enough, and had enough access to Duke to get a message to them, was Shay. "Shay must have gotten it to us. She must have."

"Is there any way it's a trap or a trick?" Rachel asked.

"It wasn't addressed to us. There's no signature. It's written in *some* kind of code. So, it might not be from your father, but it's Duke's handwriting." He cleared his throat. "As of yesterday, North Star still had Duke. It could be from North Star. They could have made him write it, but I have to believe if they went through the trouble to track us down, they would have just taken us. You especially. Or written a more specific note."

"Here. Let me see it."

He handed her the paper, though he wasn't sure what she was going to do with it. She felt the corner of the paper. "It's Dad. And not like someone made him write it, either. That's an actual note from him."

"How can you tell?"

"We developed a little system when I was in school. If he had to sign something and he'd done it, he'd poke a little hole in the corner. If there was no hole, I knew I needed to ask him again." She held up the paper, and sure enough there was a small hole in the corner. "What does it say?"

"Rachel knows the key and the lock."

Her eyebrows drew together. *"Me?"* She shook her head. "I don't know anything about that key we found. Let alone what it would unlock."

They were silent for the next few minutes, Rachel frowning as if searching her mind for an answer. Tucker studied the note again, wondering if there was more to it. Something he wasn't seeing. Something more…abstract.

He looked up at Rachel. She'd gone back to tidying up the tent. It was less smooth than how she did it at home since she was going by feel rather than lifelong knowledge of a place. Still, she had the inside of the tent all packed up in no time.

Duke thought she knew what he was talking about, Tucker assumed. Rachel didn't think she knew anything about the key or its lock.

"Maybe it's about your dream. If you know, but you don't actually *know*, maybe the answer is in your subconscious."

Chapter Thirteen

Her dream. Rachel's arms broke out in goose bumps. As much as she was slowly coming around to the idea her dream might be more reality and memory than fiction, she wasn't comfortable with her subconscious knowing something she couldn't access.

Especially when it came to this.

"Dad doesn't know anything about my dreams changing. He still thinks they're about a mountain lion."

"Did you tell him about your dreams?"

"When I was a kid. When I first started having them. He…" An uncomfortable memory had her chest tightening, like she couldn't breathe.

Tucker was immediately at her side. He rubbed a hand up and down her back. "Hey, breathe. It's all right, sweetheart. Take a deep breath."

She managed, barely. The panic had been so swift, so all encompassing, it was hard to move beyond. "I don't know if this was the first time I had the dream, but I remember being little. I still… I may have even still had the bandages on my face. Dad would sleep on the floor of my room. Mom would try to get him to come to bed, but he would insist. He said he was afraid I'd wander away again."

Tucker kept rubbing her back, and it gave her some modicum of comfort as her body seemed to chill from the inside out.

"I remember telling him about the nightmare and he told me not to tell Mom. That whenever I had nightmares or felt scared, I should tell him. Only him. He said so Mom wouldn't worry, but…"

"If your mother didn't know…"

"How…how could she have not known? How could he have lied to her? How could he have had *me* lie to her?"

"He was in WITSEC, Rach. I'm not saying it was the right thing to do, but you're supposed to leave your old life behind. Entirely."

"It's his story. The mountain lion. He made that up." The horror of that almost made her knees weak. He'd pushed her into the mountain lion story, made sure he convinced her the dreams were of that.

Even when they weren't.

"Are you sure?" Tucker asked gently.

"No. How can I be sure?" Her throat closed up and she refused to cry, but how was she expected to have an answer from a dream? "Everything is wrapped up in a dream that suddenly changed on me!"

"Hey. Maybe it's not about your dream. Maybe I've got this all wrong."

She shook her head. "You know you don't. You're a detective. You know how to piece things together."

She wrapped her arms around herself. "What else would I know that I don't think I know? You're right. It's something about my dream, but I don't know *what*."

"Okay, then let's work through this like I'd work through any case. We start at the beginning. What's the very first part of your dream you remember?"

"Do you really think the answer is in my dream?" she asked.

"I don't know. I really don't. But it might help. To lay it all out."

Rachel didn't think that was possible. She'd spent most of her life knowing this dream might pop up. Except the dream had morphed. From what Dad had pointed her to—to the truth? It was impossible to know for sure.

Maybe she'd never get rid of the nightmares, but maybe she could find the truth in the way it had changed… Maybe.

"I'm not sure I know where to start," she said, her voice rough and her chest tight.

Tucker's arm came around her shoulders and he gave her an affectionate squeeze. "Sit. No use crouching around."

"No, no. I need to…to move. To be doing something."

"Okay, so we'll go out and break down the tent while you talk. Sound good?"

She nodded. He helped lead her outside, then led her to the first stake.

"Do you mind if I do it myself?"

"Whatever you need, Rach."

She nodded once and pulled out the stake. Then she felt around the tent, slowly taking it apart. She didn't like to camp, but she and Sarah had often put tents up and down around the ranch as forts or playhouses, so she was familiar with the process of breaking down the tent even without her sight.

Tucker didn't push. He didn't ask questions. Nor did he jump in to help take down the tent. He waited until she started to speak herself. "I'm not sure I know exactly where it starts. When I wake up, when I try to remember, it's just that I'm suddenly aware I'm being carried away."

"Carried away from where?"

"Home. I don't see home, but I know he's taking me away from home." Even knowing she was safe with Tucker, the fear and panic clawed at her. She focused on the tent. "He's taking me away from… lights. I think there's a light behind us and he's going into the dark."

"Lights on in the house maybe?"

"I think so." Even though it was silly since she couldn't see anyway, she closed her eyes. She tried to bring the nightmare back to her. She'd seen for the first three years of her life. There were things she could remember, and this dream had always been one of them.

"Or maybe it's the stables." She opened her eyes, frowning. She could tell light was beginning to dawn in the here and now, but she still couldn't fully make out Tucker's shape. "It isn't windows. It isn't a glow

like if it was home at dark. It's more one lone beam
of light. I think it's the light outside the stables."

"So, he's taking you away from the stables,"
Tucker said. His voice was calm and serious and
believing. He took everything she said at face value
and put it into the puzzle they were trying to work
out. "The light on the stables is on the north side. If
you're moving straight away from it, that's heading
into the north pasture."

"Or toward the highway." She felt how *right* it
was, more than saw or knew. Going away from one
lone light, heading for the dark of the highway. "The
new dream, the changed dream, he's holding me so
tight I can barely breathe. I'm too scared to scream.
He's talking, but I can't make sense of the words. In
my head, they're just a jumble. I just want my mom."

Tears welled up because she still just wanted
Mom and couldn't have her. Couldn't find comfort
in her. She'd been gone for so many years now. Rachel folded the tent poles and blinked back tears,
fought to make her voice steady. She appreciated
that Tucker didn't rush her.

"At some point I notice eyes watching us. They
glow a little."

"Mountain lion?"

"At first, that's what I thought. As me. Adult me."
She frowned. "I think Dad convinced me that's what
I was seeing when I told him about the dream. But
when I think about how I saw the eyes move, how
it jumps out… I think it was a dog. We used to have
dogs then. Lots of them."

"Yeah, four or five, right?"

Rachel nodded. "If this is all real—if it isn't my three-year-old brain getting things mixed up, or dreams mixing with reality, I think it was one of the dogs."

"And it just follows you while the man is carrying you away?"

"Yes. I'm not scared of the eyes. I'm scared of the man. He's holding me too tight, and he has…" She trailed off. This was where she didn't want to go, even knowing she had to.

"Last time, you said he had some kind of knife."

Rachel nodded, folding the tent with shaking hands. "It's either a knife with prongs, or multiple knives. It's sharp, and it keeps flashing in the moonlight." She brought a hand to her scars, and could feel the smooth lines. "It could have made this. Not claws, but this special knife he's carrying." Her breath whooshed out of her. "How is it possible?" she whispered. "And what does any of that tell us about a key?"

"I don't know yet, but let's focus on what you do remember. On the dream."

"That's all I remember. The last one I had, the one where he actually cut me? That's the first time I remember getting that far. Even when I was a kid, he never hurt me in my dream. I woke up before. But in this one, the dog jumps out. The man slashes the knife down and it cuts into me. I can feel the pain and the blood, and hear the dog—barking and snarling. But the dog isn't the one hurting me."

Tucker collected the tent and the poles. She could hear him wrapping it all up and putting it into his backpack. He said nothing.

"Thank you for letting me take down the tent."

"Thank you?"

"Most people can't stand to watch me do something myself, at a slower pace than they would go. They have to jump in to help to speed things up."

"We've got all the time in the world right now, Rach."

But Tucker didn't understand that time didn't always matter. People's compulsion with accomplishing tasks made it hard for them to step back. So, she'd just appreciated that he hadn't needed to do that.

He didn't press about the key, or if she remembered any more of her dream. He simply gave her the space to work through it.

"Do you know where my father is? Where they're keeping him or hiding him or whatever?"

"No."

"Would Cody know?"

Tucker hesitated. "It's possible."

"I don't have the answer to this, Tuck. And Dad clearly wants me to, or thinks I do. He sent us a message, and if Shay was the messenger, it probably wasn't sanctioned by your group."

"No, probably not."

"I need to talk to him. It's the only way."

TUCKER COULDN'T LET his own personal feelings or issues, as she'd call them, rule his thoughts or actions.

Though it was hard to ignore how much it hurt, he couldn't do this without bringing his brother into the fold.

His brother who'd actually fought the Sons. On multiple levels. And won. Beat Ace. Beat those who would have hurt Cody and his daughter.

Cody. His *baby* brother.

"Tucker?"

"Sorry. I'm just trying to figure out how that would work. We'd have to get to a place that has cell service, and we don't know for sure that North Star doesn't have ways of tracking your phone, too."

"Maybe we should head back to the ranch. Surely North Star doesn't think we'll go back. They'll think we're on the run. We go back. Get word to someone without phones, and have Cody meet us somewhere? We could hide on the ranch. That's smart, don't you think?"

Tucker had to pause and work very hard to keep the bitterness out of his voice. "Yeah, smart."

"Unless you have a better plan?"

"No, Rachel. I don't." How could he?

He continued to clean up the campsite, leaving Rachel standing there with her cane. She ran her fingers over her horse's mane.

She made quite a picture there, dark hand moving through the cream-colored mane of the horse. Her hair was a mess, but it haloed her face. The sun was rising behind her, making the rolling hills sparkle like some kind of fairyland. Her, the reigning queen of it all.

She made a face. "I can tell you're staring at me."

"Maybe I'm staring at the scenery."

"Maybe. But I don't think you are. Why are you staring at me, Tuck?"

"Maybe I think you're pretty, Rach." Which wasn't what he should have said, even if he meant it. Even if her looking pretty was something akin to a punch in the gut. There wasn't room for this—not just because of the current situation—but because of the *always* situation.

"You could kiss me again," she said, very seriously.

She had no idea what it cost him to sound unaffected. "I could, but I don't think that's such a good idea."

"Why not?"

"I can't imagine what Duke would say if I happened to mention it took us so long to help him because I was busy making out with his daughter after spending the night in a tent together."

"After keeping me from being taken by this North Star Group, who are supposedly good guys but condone kidnapping." She huffed out a breath. "I don't understand why you joined them in the first place. Why you worked for people who made you lie."

"Sometimes lies aren't the worst thing in the world."

"I suppose not, but you're not comfortable with them. The weight of that guilt weighs a little heavier on you."

She was right, somehow always seeing right through him. Which meant it seemed honesty was the only option—especially if it kept him from talking about kissing.

"I've been working with them because… I thought I could do something. My father never thought much of me. Not as a threat or as a successor, and mostly I've been grateful for that. But I thought I could do something, like Cody and Jamison did. Like Gage and Brady did. Hell, even Dev stood up to him." He scowled. It hadn't ended well for Dev at all, but he'd tried. "I've done nothing. I thought I could be a piece of what brought my father down, so I did what North Star asked even though it hurt."

She dropped her hand from the horse, used her probing cane to move forward until she was close to him. Too close. "Until they wanted to take me." She looked up at him, her eyes dark except where they were damaged.

To think it had been a man not a mountain lion made it all worse somehow. The end result was the same, but someone had done that to her on purpose. When she'd only been three. All because her father had done the right thing decades ago.

"You didn't deserve to be dragged into this."

"No. I'm not sure you did, either." She reached out, resting her hand on his arm.

He wanted to touch her hair, her face. He wanted to somehow take those scars away from her, which was a stupid want. This was the life they had. He could only make the right decisions now.

Which meant he had to keep his hands off her. "The Sons connect to me. They connect to this. Don't they always?"

"Only if you let them." She moved onto her toes,

leaned into him. She brushed her lips across his jaw, though he imagined she'd been going for his cheek or mouth. Still, it rippled through him. No matter how he told himself to block it away.

"Dev'd probably be a better option for all this," he said, voice tight. She'd be good for Dev. All light and hope to his dark and hopeless.

She wrinkled her nose and fell back onto her flat feet. "Dev's even older than *you*. And so grouchy. Dev is better suited for a life of inherent bachelorhood. Grandma Pauline told me once all her uncles were bachelors, and she wouldn't be surprised if the lot of you ended up just like them."

"Did she now. Well, four out of six proved her wrong, didn't they?"

"You won't be a perennial bachelor, Tucker. You're too sweet."

"Gee. Thanks."

"You think that's some kind of slight, but it's a compliment. It's a miracle, actually. The way you were brought up. To have any sweet. I think that's pretty amazing."

She almost made him believe it.

"We should get back. Time isn't on our side. The North Star Group has a lot of skills, technology and reach. We can only avoid them for so long, even with Shay's help."

"All right, but you're not getting out of this so easy."

No, he didn't think he was.

Chapter Fourteen

The ride back to the ranch was quiet. Not tense, exactly. There was a certain comfort to just riding Buttercup, Tucker's strong body behind her. A companionable silence as they both thought through what was next.

She had to believe Cody would know enough about North Star to figure out where they'd be keeping her father or what they'd be doing with him. She had to believe he'd give them the location, Tucker would find Dad, and they'd get him away.

Then what?

Well, the key. Dad would know what the key opened and maybe it would…end everything.

Of course, she thought if it would end everything Dad would have handed it over to North Star, told *them* about the key and the lock. But maybe he just didn't trust them. Maybe he could only trust her.

Rachel wished she had any idea what the key was for. There was nothing to unlock in her dream. There was only darkness and fear. Pain and relief all mixed into one powerful, messy, emotional experience.

Tucker zigzagged through rolling hills. "I'm going to head up along the north pasture, come down to the stables that way. Maybe the route will remind you of something."

"I can't see, Tucker."

"I know, Rachel," he said with an endless patience that dug at her. "But I'll tell you where we are, what I see. It can't hurt to try to reenact the moment. And if it doesn't jog your memory, all we've done is add a little time I would have probably added anyway to make sure we aren't being followed."

She didn't say anything to that. Going through the dream once already had left her emotionally drained. Then there was the fact Tucker had refused to kiss her.

Though she wasn't convinced it was because he didn't *want* to. She figured there was something more about honor or loving her dad or something twisted up. Because he watched her. She couldn't see and she could *tell* he looked at her in ways he hadn't before.

She could feel the tension in him when she'd touched him. That quick little sigh of breath he'd tried to hide when she'd tried to kiss his mouth and ended up just touching her lips to his jaw.

Maybe she'd missed, but that had been nice, too. The rough whiskers against her lips. There had been an exciting friction in that.

Tucker Wyatt and exciting friction. She might have laughed at the thought of those two things going together, but it just seemed…right, when it never had before.

"We're on the hill outside the north pasture gate. I can see the top of the stable. From here I can see the light. If it was dark and the light was on, it'd be visible this whole stretch."

Even though she didn't want to, she brought to mind her dream. The light. "Where's the highway in relation to where we are?"

"We're facing south. The highway is due east."

"And how far would you be able to see the light in that direction?"

He clicked to the horse, and they moved. "Let's see. If you were headed for the highway, but looking back toward the house or stables…" He trailed off and the horse moved in a gently swaying motion beneath them. "Most of the way. The main gate is just coming into view and I can see the very top of it. Which means if the light was on, I'd be able to see it clearer."

The main gate led to a gravel road, which led to the highway, but it all made sense. The light had gotten smaller as the man had taken her. Like it was slowly being enveloped—or in this case, hidden by distance, direction and hills.

"I think that's where he was taking me."

"On foot, right? So, probably heading for a vehicle. Then the dog saves you."

Rachel brought a hand up to her scars. Her mother had never let her feel much self-pity over the loss of sight, over the scars. Rachel supposed her age helped with that. She didn't remember all that much before, so it wasn't a comparison or ruminating over what she'd lost.

But the dog *saving* her felt like too strong a word. She hadn't been saved fully. She'd lost something that night.

"Tuck…" She swallowed at the sudden emotion clogging her throat. "Why do you think he did it? Lied to me. To my mom. Made us think something had happened when it hadn't. I know he had to keep his former life a secret, but… I love him, I do. Nothing changes that, but I'm having a really hard time not being mad at him for warping my nightmares to keep this secret."

"Can you imagine how he feels? He did something right. *One right thing.* He did his job, and he had to leave his entire life. Then he starts a new one and this right thing he did not only haunts him, it hurts and permanently injures his daughter. I lied to you, Rach. Because I thought it would protect you. You and Sarah and…everyone. I can't imagine his lies were any different."

"But they are. He made me think something completely different happened than actually did. It wasn't just a lie of omission or hiding something. He *warped* something I actually experienced."

"What's worse? Believing a random act of Mother Nature hurt you, or that your father's past was out there, just waiting? I know what that's like. To know at any point your past could pop up and ruin your life. I mean, Grandma Pauline gave us a good life, a good childhood once we got out of the Sons. But we always knew Ace could pop up—hurt us, hurt her. We always knew Jamison sacrificed eighteen years to get us out of there. It's a hard, heavy weight."

Rachel didn't know what to say to that. She certainly couldn't argue with it, and as much as it hurt that her father had lied to her in such a devious way, she understood that Tucker thought Duke had given her a gift. Maybe he had. What would life have been like if she'd always been afraid?

Tucker had come through it okay, but she was realizing he had deeper scars than he ever let on.

Tucker's body went suddenly tense, not just behind her but his arms holding the reins around her. Everything in him was iron and she was encompassed in all that strength. "We're going to get off the horse."

"What? Why? What's happened?"

"There's a man watching us." He'd slowed down Buttercup, but they were still moving. "We have to do this quickly. I'm going to swing you off with me. I'll point you in the right direction. Then you run for the stables. I'll send Buttercup off as a distraction, and I'll run for him. Three different directions, and he'll either focus on the horse or me."

"Is it North Star?"

Tucker was quiet for a long moment. "I want you to run to the stables. Hide in there. That's it."

"But—"

"I need you to do it, Rach. If I need help, I'll yell, okay?"

He wouldn't. She knew he wouldn't. But he couldn't protect himself, or her, if she didn't listen to him. He'd try to play the hero even more than he already was.

If he wasn't answering her question about North Star, well, that was worse. So, she'd run. If she made it to the stables, she could make it to the house. She could call for help. She didn't have her cane, but once she got to the stables she'd know where she was. She'd be able to move around the ranch without it.

As long as she didn't fall on her run to the stables.

"On my count. One, two, three." She let him swing her off the horse, and he helped her land a lot more gracefully than she might have alone. He turned her by the shoulders in the right direction.

Then, she ran.

TUCKER POINTED RACHEL in the right direction, gave Buttercup's reins a flick, then ran himself. There was no cover until he got a lot closer, so he couldn't pretend like he was doing anything but going after the man behind the fence.

Who had a gun. If it was North Star, he wouldn't shoot.

If it wasn't…well…

The sound of the gunshot had him hitting the ground. When nothing hit him, he took a chance to look toward Rachel. She was still running, as was Buttercup, so no one had been struck.

Tucker got back to his feet, went back to running toward the man, but this time in a zigzag pattern. If he could get to the copse of trees that followed the creek, he could use some cover to get closer.

Another gunshot. Tucker didn't dive for the ground this time. Based on the angle of the gun, he was almost certain the man was shooting at him, not the horse or Rachel. He didn't have time to pause and look, though. He had to keep going.

He reached the cluster of trees and pulled his gun out of its holster. Clicking the safety off, he gave himself a moment to hide behind a tree and steady his breathing. His chest burned with effort, his heart pounded with fear and adrenaline.

The creek was nearly dry, but the trees were thick and old. When the third gunshot went off, it hit a tree way too close to Tucker for comfort.

The fence the man had been crouched behind was due east of the tree Tucker was behind. Still, moving enough to see and shoot would put him at risk.

It was only a gut feeling, not fact, but Tucker sincerely doubted the man was part of North Star. As much as they might prioritize mission over innocent life, they weren't the type to shoot first and ask questions later.

That was more Sons territory. But what would they be doing just lurking around waiting for Tucker and Rachel to appear? How would they know they'd disappeared in the first place?

Unless it was coincidence.

Tucker couldn't mull it over much longer. He had to act so whoever the gunman was didn't get it in his head to go after Rachel.

He slid from one tree to another, working the angles to keep as much distance between him and the shooter as possible.

Another shot went off, but it was way more off target than the last one. Tucker got the glimpse of movement out of the corner of his eye, quickly changed direction to get behind a tree. The gunman was coming toward him just as Tucker tried to move toward the gunman.

He was somewhat hesitant to shoot someone not knowing where they came from or why they were shooting at him, but when the next bullet hit the tree he was standing behind, he figured it was time to do what needed to be done.

Tucker used the tree as cover, listened for the man's movements, then when he thought he had a clear idea of where the man was, stuck his arm out to shoot. He didn't need it to hit, just needed to catch the man off guard.

Immediately after the first shot, he peeked out from behind the tree. The shooter had ducked behind a bush, but as he slowly rose again, gun aimed, Tucker managed to get off a shot first.

The man stumbled backward. Tucker immediately charged. He didn't think he'd hit anything vital, which meant he had to get the gun away from him.

The assailant had lost his gun—a long high-powered looking model—after Tucker had shot him, but he was curling his fingers around the barrel as Tucker approached. He had to lunge to get to it before the man could lift it.

It was narrow timing, but Tucker managed to grab a hold of the handle. They grappled, pulling and jerking like a life-or-death game of tug-of-war. Which gave Tucker the idea to take the dangerous chance of letting the gun go.

Since he'd been pulling hard, the attacker fell backward, the gun winging out of his grasp as Tucker had hoped. Tucker immediately leaped on him.

Even with the gunshot wound, the man fought hard. The bullet must have only glanced his side, even with the amount of blood staining his shirt. Tucker had to fight dirty to win, so he landed the hardest blow he could at the spot with the most blood.

The man howled, grabbing the injured section and rolling away. Tucker managed to pin him, face down, hands pulled behind his back. With pressure on the injured side to keep the man from fighting back, Tucker looked around for something to tie the man's hands.

Which was when he noticed the man was wearing a utility belt. Tucker went through the pockets, found a phone and tossed it as far into the creek bed as he could. Next he discovered a plastic bottle of some kind of clear liquid wrapped in a cloth—he disposed of that in the same way—and then happened upon the perfect answer to his problems. Zip ties. He quickly got them on the man's wrists, then had to fight to get another one around the man's legs.

The man swore and spit and kicked, but there wasn't much he could do with his arms tied behind his back and his legs bound together. Tucker got to his feet and rolled the man over onto his back.

Tucker didn't recognize him—not that he'd recognize every Sons goon. Still, there was something different about him. About the way he dressed and held himself, as though he wasn't quite used to the rough terrain.

Sons members were too local, too used to living in the elements and outside of society. This man didn't even have a knife on him. Just the high-powered gun, some zip ties, the phone and a tiny bottle of something Tucker assumed was a knock-out drug.

All the tools for kidnapping.

Tucker's stomach roiled, but he didn't let it show. He sneered down at the man.

"I assume you're with Vianni."

The man spit at him.

Tucker didn't flinch, didn't jump away, as the spit missed him entirely. He kept his sole focus on the assailant. "Who are you here for?"

"Not you."

"I guess I could just leave you here, all tied up, and never let anyone know." Tucker looked up at the sky. "Might be fall, but sunny day like this? Going to get pretty hot."

"Bud, so much worse is coming for you if you don't let me go. I don't even care *what* you do."

Tucker leaned in, smiled. "Oh, you're going to care."

Chapter Fifteen

The gunshots had Rachel pulling out her phone. She was afraid to speak too loudly, but her phone was having trouble picking up her voice with her shaky whisper. "Call Cody," she finally said with enough force.

"Rachel? Where are you?"

There was a sharp command in his voice that calmed her. Because he would know what to do when she didn't.

"I'm in the stables at our ranch. Tucker saw someone and went after them. There's been gunshots. I know you're in Bonesteel—"

"I'm going to get off the line and call Brady. He's right next door."

"No! Listen. I mean, you can call Brady, but you have to know North Star is mixed up in this somehow. They have Dad. Tucker was working for them. Then this woman helped us—helped *me* not get taken by North Star and… I don't understand what's going on."

There was a brief pause. "I'm calling Brady to

help Tuck. As for North Star…" Another pause that had Rachel holding her breath. "The woman? Was her name Shay?"

"Yes."

"All right. You stay put. I'll get back to you on the North Star thing." The connection clicked off and Rachel slipped her phone back into her pocket. Sure, Brady could maybe take care of things, but he was hurt, too. Likely Dev was out in the pasture somewhere with Sarah.

Would they have heard the gunshots? Surely, they'd have had to. Wouldn't they come running? Call their own reinforcements?

She couldn't just stand here, though. Tuck could have been the one shot.

She heard the door creak open and she pressed herself against the corner.

"Rach?"

"Tuck." She raced forward too quickly and tripped, but arms grabbed her before she could fall face-first. She was too relieved he was okay to be embarrassed. She held on to him as he helped her back to her feet. "You're okay."

"Yeah. We have to get out of here."

"No, it's okay. I phoned Cody. He was calling Brady and figuring out the North Star thing and—"

"What did you do that for?" he demanded, his voice sharp and unforgiving. He released her and she stood in the middle of the stable, feeling unaccountably chastened.

"What do you mean, what did I do that for? A

man was out there. I heard gunshots. What was I supposed to do?"

"Just hide here like I told you to."

"You don't get to boss me around, Tuck. Certainly not when there are *guns* going off. We agreed to talk to Cody about—"

"About where your dad might be. Not drag my brothers into a lethal situation."

"Why not? You got dragged into Brady's thing. Brady was dragged into Felicity's. It's what we do. Get dragged into each other's dangerous run-ins. And it always goes a little better with help, doesn't it?"

He was silent.

"Besides, it's too late. Cody is calling Brady and he's going to look into the North Star thing. He knows Shay."

"Well, he used to work for them."

"But he knew who she was even before I said her name."

"Sit tight," Tucker said, like he was about to leave her alone again. *Oh, no. Not going to happen.* She lunged forward and managed to grab his shirt.

"You will stop this right now." He tried to tug her hand off his shirt, but she only held on tighter. "I don't know what the damn key unlocks, Tucker. I don't understand anything Dad said in that letter. Now there's a man after us. Don't brush me off. Don't tell me to sit tight, and don't act like a child because we need help. I can't even do the *one thing* Dad seems to think I can." Emotion rose up in her throat, making her words squeak when it was the last thing she wanted. "If we need help, it's because of me. Not you."

"Rach." Instead of tugging her hand away again, he drew her close and smoothed a hand over her hair. "None of this is your fault."

Wouldn't that be nice? She leaned into Tucker, wondering if she'd ever fully believe that when the letter had said she was the key. It helped that he'd said it, though. That he'd take the time to give her a hug.

Someone cleared their throat from over by the door. "Uh, sorry to interrupt but I was just wondering if I should ask why there's a guy in zip ties lying next to the creek?" Dev said.

"What are you doing here?" Tucker demanded, releasing her abruptly.

"What am I doing here? You know how sound travels, right? Gunshots ring out while I'm tending to my cattle, and I'm left figuring out who the hell is shooting things. I sent Sarah over to Grandma's to round up help."

"Tucker's being very childish about help."

Dev made a sound that *might* have been a laugh, if he wasn't perpetually grumpy Dev who almost never laughed. At least not without a sarcastic edge. "Yeah, we Wyatts get that way sometimes. Should I leave the guy where he is?"

"Yes," Tucker said.

"And there aren't others?"

"Not yet."

"Who is he?" Rachel demanded.

There was a pause and Rachel didn't have to see to know *something* passed between brothers.

"I guess I'll go head over and stop Sarah and Brady and whoever else off at the pass."

"Have Brady call local police—ones he'd trust to keep it as quiet as possible—to pick up the guy."

Dev didn't say anything to that, but she heard him retreating so she assumed it was some kind of assent.

"What exactly are we going to do?"

"We're going to follow the original plan. Sort of. The next step is getting Cody to see what he might be able to tell us about North Star and Duke, but I want to keep the rest of the family out of it as much as we can. Not because I need to do this on my own, but because the more people we drag into this, the more targets they have. The wider it gets, the harder it is to fight."

She supposed that made sense. A gunman had been waiting on the ranch. What if Sarah had happened to drive by on her way to town? Or what if Dev had come that way instead of across the pasture where Knight land butted up against Reaves land?

If she and Tucker went off on their own, maybe they'd be able to keep the focus on them, not their families.

"So, we're heading to Bonesteel on Buttercup?"

"Not exactly. The guy has to have a car around here somewhere. And it just so happens, I grabbed his keys."

TUCKER LED RACHEL toward the front gate. He imagined Vianni's man had hidden the car somewhere on the gravel road. There weren't very many places to hide a car, so it should be easy enough to find.

"It still doesn't make sense," Rachel said, one arm hooked with his as he helped her walk. Though this ground was a little more familiar than not, she didn't spend a lot of time walking this far past the main buildings.

"What doesn't?"

"Dad's note. I've gone over and over my dream. There's never been anything about a key. Or a lock. Not in old dreams and not in the new ones. Dad wouldn't even know about the new ones. I never mentioned it to anyone until you. In fact, the more I think about it, the more I don't think he knew I still had the nightmares. I didn't tell him. I didn't wake up screaming. For all he knew, they went away."

It made Tucker's chest ache that she'd continued to be tormented by the dreams and hadn't told Duke, or anyone else. Just dealt with them. As they slowly morphed into something real.

"What else could it be?"

She shook her head as they walked. "I don't know, but we've only focused on my dream. Maybe it's something else…"

"Okay, so the note said you know the key and the lock. We've been focusing on the key, since we found that. Maybe we should think about locks. Are there any locks in your dream?"

She shook her head. "No keys. No locks. Nothing even symbolic of a key or a lock."

"So let's think about Duke. Do you remember

anything about keys and locks you specifically associate with him?"

They reached the gate and Tucker looked down the gravel lane. He wanted to get out of here before the police arrived. Avoid answering any questions they'd have so he and Rachel could move on to the next step.

He wasn't looking forward to bringing Cody into this, but there didn't seem to be another option. Brady was involved now. Dev as well, to an extent.

It ate at him that he'd failed so spectacularly at keeping them out of it. He'd wanted to let them heal and protect their families and instead…

"Wait." Rachel stopped abruptly. "Key and lock. It wouldn't have to be…literal, would it?"

"I mean, we have a key. That's pretty literal."

"Or it's not. It's not about the dream. It's not about the key. It's about Dad. Take me to the cemetery."

"I'm sorry…*what*?"

"The cemetery. Where Mom's buried. It's not far from here. Dad always said… Mom was the key to his lock. Like, always. It was one of his favorite sayings before she died. He doesn't say it much anymore. But he used to. Key and lock."

"Okay," Tucker said gently. "But…"

"Maybe it's nothing. I know it sounds crazy. But Dad wrote that letter and it says, *Rachel knows the key and the lock*. Well, if he's the lock—she's the key."

Tucker couldn't imagine what might be hiding at the cemetery, let alone at Eva Knight's grave, but it was hard to refuse her request. Even knowing it was beyond a long shot.

"We have to find the car first." He opened the gate and led Rachel through. The Knight ranch was the last turn off on the gravel road. If Tucker had been trying to hide a car, he'd have gone past the gate, then tried to hide the car in a ditch.

They walked down the side, Tucker keeping an eye and ear out for any cars that might be coming.

Just as he'd predicted, he found the car just a ways down, half in a ditch. You'd only see it if you passed the gate and likely their little spy had been counting on no one going that far.

Tucker helped Rachel into the car, then slid into the driver's seat himself, adjusting the seat. It smelled a little too much like cigarettes and cheap cologne, so he rolled down the windows.

Keeping his eye out for a police cruiser, he took the backroads to the cemetery where Eva Knight was buried. The parking lot was empty, which was good. "We can't spend too much time here."

"I know. I just need to… I don't know. If she's the key…"

"I get it." He thought it was too symbolic and metaphorical, but she had to look. Hell, even he had to look or he'd wonder if he'd missed something. He got out of the car, then went over to Rachel's side and helped her out, leading her through the archway of the cemetery entrance.

He didn't have to lead her any farther than that. She'd clearly been here plenty, since she walked around the other graves with unerring accuracy, before stopping in front of her mother's.

Eva Knight. Loving wife and mother to all her girls. 1970–2006.

She'd been more than that little epitaph. She'd been the only calm, gentle presence across the Knight and Wyatt ranches. Until Rachel had taken on that mantle, and maybe Tucker had tried to be some of that as much as he could.

"I miss her," Rachel said softly.

"Me too." Missed her, and felt suddenly ashamed he'd let Rachel get so involved in this. Eva would have expected him to keep her safe. Keep *all* the girls safe. "She'd want you to be safe. At home."

"No. No, she wouldn't." Rachel smiled at him, and though there were tears in her eyes, they didn't fall. "She wanted everyone to treat me like an equal. Even if it hadn't been for the blindness, I was their only biological daughter and she never wanted the other girls to feel less. She was careful. So careful to treat me like everyone else. To give me the same responsibilities and expectations. Honestly, I think that's why… Well, Dad and Sarah, they kind of treat me like a maid. They don't mean to. It's just, I was always supposed to pull my weight. Mom wanted me on equal footing." She took a deep shaky breath. "I *am* on equal footing. Maybe you have the eyes and the police skills, but I know the key and the lock. What do you see?"

"Just the grave. Just the grass around it. There are some flowers in the holder."

"Fresh?"

"Yeah, they're drooping a bit. Maybe been here a few days, but fresh enough."

"So, Dad's been here recently. Before he left."

"It could have been one of your sisters."

She shook her head. "No. They always tell me if they're going so I can go, too. It had to be Dad. And it was in the last few days. The key *has* to be here."

Tucker didn't remind her that technically they had a key, and they were essentially just searching for a lock. Still, he would do it for her because... Well, his leads were nonexistent. He went around the grave, looking for anything. He even pulled out the flowers and looked into the water holder. He laid his hands over the stone, and it was only as he moved his palm over the side of the grave that he felt something odd under his foot.

Unsure, he stood. "Wait. This is..." Tucker toed the grass with his boot. A whole section of it moved, like a square of sod had been placed down over dirt. Coincidence, no doubt. Still he let go of Rachel and crouched down. He pulled up the square of sod. Underneath was freshly unpacked dirt. Tucker poked his finger into it. Not far beneath the crumbles of dirt was something hard.

"What is it?" Rachel demanded.

He began to dig in earnest. It was just a tiny metal tube, but it had a lid and Tucker screwed it off. He pulled out a slip of paper. It only had numbers on it, but it was clear what they were. "I found a piece of paper buried in the ground. There are numbers on it. It's a combination. Like to a safe."

"The only safe I know of is…"

"Grandma Pauline's," they finished together.

Chapter Sixteen

They drove to Reaves ranch in silence. Rachel felt a little raw as she always did after visiting her mother's grave. She'd only been seven when Mom had died, but she had worked so hard to live up to that memory that it felt like her mom had been around longer.

Which was nice.

It was also strange that Tucker had said Eva would have expected him to keep her safe, and suddenly she understood her place in her family a little better. Mom had done her best to make her an equal for two very different reasons—biology and her blindness—and both had worked. She was an independent, equal individual in her family.

If she'd felt trapped before this all started, or scared her future was never going to change, maybe that was just normal adulthood stuff—not the result of her blindness.

"What are we going to do?" Tucker muttered. "Just barge in and demand Grandma Pauline let us open her safe?"

Rachel didn't think he was actually asking her,

but she answered anyway. "She knows something, Tuck. If this leads to *her* safe, Dad certainly didn't hide it there without her knowing."

She could sense his frustration. She wasn't sure exactly what it was toward, so she reached over and rested her hand on his arm. It was tense, and she imagined he was gripping the steering wheel hard enough to break it.

"If Grandma hid something about this, you should be angry with her," he told her.

"I'll save my anger for when I know what actually happened. You're only angry because you're scared."

"Scared?" he demanded.

"Your brothers can take care of themselves, even if they're injured or have kids to protect. You have a certain comfort in knowing they're all law enforcement and know how to deal with these issues. But your grandmother?"

"Raised the six of us, put the fear of God into Ace so he never came after her, and taught us all how to shoot way better than any law enforcement training. I'm not scared for her."

Rachel wasn't so sure. Sometimes you could know someone was strong and good, like her father, and still worry something had changed. Or something had been there that you'd never known.

She sighed as Tucker slowed the car. "How are we going to play this?"

"We're going to go in and tell her we're going to open the safe."

"You've met your grandmother, right? You go in

there demanding things, she's going to knock you out with that wooden spoon."

Tucker didn't say anything to that, so she opened the car door and slid out. "You let me handle it," she said decisively. She closed the car door and started striding for the house. Tucker hadn't parked in his normal spot, so once she reached the house she had to feel around for the door.

She didn't knock. She stepped inside, and she could hear Tucker striding quickly behind her as if he meant to beat her to the house and take over.

No. Not on this. "Grandma Pauline?"

"What on earth are you doing here?" Pauline demanded.

Rachel could make out her form over by the sink or oven. "We need to get into the safe."

Tucker closed the door behind her, and she could feel him standing next to her. She couldn't see Grandma Pauline's expression, but she could feel the hesitation in the silence.

Rachel nodded toward Tucker. "We have the combination. Because Dad gave us a clue. He wants us to get into the safe."

Grandma Pauline sighed. "All right, then. Follow me."

"That wasn't exactly asking nicely," Tucker muttered into her ear. He took her arm as if he meant to lead her, and though she didn't need it in this house, she didn't mind her arm in his hand.

"I can say things like that to her. *You* can't," Rachel whispered back as Grandma Pauline led them down into the basement.

Rachel had to trust Grandma Pauline and Tucker to open the safe. To tell her what was inside. She knew from hearing everyone talk about it that it was a giant safe. The boys used to joke it was where Grandma Pauline hid dead bodies.

Rachel shuddered at the thought.

"Bottom shelf there. That's Duke's," Grandma Pauline said in her no-nonsense way.

Tucker let go of her elbow. There was the sound of shuffling and scraping. "It's another safe," Tucker said, sounding wholly baffled. "Not small, either. What on earth is happening here?"

"Is it another combination?"

"No. This one has a lock. I'm assuming that's what the key you found is for."

"Well, open it," she urged. Surely this safe wouldn't lead to yet another. *Surely* this was the last step.

Rachel had to wait more interminable seconds. She could hear Tucker fitting the key into the hole on the lock. The click. A squeak as the safe opened.

Tucker swore. Not angrily but more shock. More…fear. Rachel even heard Grandma Pauline's sharp inhale of surprise.

"What is it?" Rachel demanded when no one spoke.

"Rachel…"

"Tell me," she insisted. "*Now.*"

Tucker sighed. "It looks like… It looks like the

knife you described in your dream. And there's… there's old blood on it."

Rachel couldn't even make sense of that. "I don't understand."

"He kept the weapon that injured you. Kept it locked away." There was a ribbon of hurt in Tucker's voice that finally made the words sink in.

Except, how…

"He kept the knife. That hurt me. On purpose."

"You knew," Tucker accused, and Rachel understood he was talking to Grandma Pauline.

"No. Not in the way you think," Grandma Pauline replied. Though she didn't betray any emotion, she didn't speak with her usual verve. "After the accident, Duke was distraught. He needed… Well, he felt alone. Guilty. Responsible. Now, you've both dealt with the Sons enough to know that it wasn't his fault. It was those awful people's fault."

It was an admonition disguised as fact—Grandma Pauline's specialty. It didn't make Rachel feel any better about anything, though.

"He asked me to hide something for him and not to ask questions. I didn't. He called it insurance. That's all I know about it. Timing-wise, I knew it connected to what happened to Rachel, but not how or what."

"It doesn't make sense. If he had what hurt me, he would have taken it to the police. He would have used it." She turned toward Tucker's form. "Why wouldn't he have used what he could to put them in jail with this when it happened?"

"I don't know, Rach."

He sounded immeasurably sad, which of course made her feel worse. Dad had kept a weapon that had blinded her at the age of three. Locked it up like he was protecting the people who'd hurt her.

"I know it's hard, but let's not jump to conclusions."

"Not jump to conclusions?" Rachel couldn't tell where Grandma Pauline was standing in the dark with her own heart beating so loud in her ears. "I was blinded by a man with that knife when I was *three years old*. I might have been killed. I'll jump to every damn conclusion I want."

And because all she wanted to do was cry, she marched back the way she'd come and up the stairs.

"WELL, DON'T JUST stand there, boy. Go follow her."

"Grandma…" Tucker couldn't wrap his head around it. He didn't know how this could have gotten so much worse. "This is…"

"You don't know *what* it is. And before you get all high and mighty on me, I don't know what it is, either. I took the safe and put it in my own because a friend asked me to. I didn't ask any questions, because I'd been around enough to understand some things are better left alone."

"He made her believe—and all of us believe—she'd been mauled by an animal."

"Any person who'd use that knife on a child *is* an animal. That's the truth of it. You don't know Duke's truth or what he's done or escaped or how this might have been him protecting her. Don't you think I've done some shady things to protect you and your brothers?"

It was a horrible thought. She'd raised them to do what was right. To uphold the law after watching their father break it, try to destroy it for the entirety of their childhoods. And she was admitting to *shady* things to keep them safe.

"Rachel's hurting. She feels betrayed. Fair enough. But you're protecting her, which means you've got to think beyond her hurt. Duke's a good man. You know it and I know it."

"Maybe he's not as good as we think he is."

"Or maybe, good isn't as simple as you want it to be. Now, go after her."

Tucker did as he was told, in part because it was habit and in part because he was worried what Rachel would do next. *He* knew what it was like to feel like you could never understand or believe in your father, but she never had.

She wasn't in the kitchen and the door was ajar, so he stepped outside. She was pacing the yard. He had a feeling that constant movement was what kept her from losing the battle with tears.

"We need to keep moving. Stay on plan."

She shook her head. "The plan? To save him from those people when he…" She just kept shaking her head as if she could negate the truth. "He shouldn't have that. I can't think of one good reason he'd have it locked up."

"Then let's go find out the reason," Tucker said gently. "We find your father. We have our answers."

"What if the answers are… What if he's…"

She couldn't get the words out, so he supplied them for her. "Not the man you thought he was?"

Her lips trembled, but she gave a sharp nod.

"Nothing he's done changes two very simple facts. One, we know he helped bring down dirty cops. Whatever he's done, he fought for the right thing and probably out of a need to protect his family. Two, he's been a great father and a good man for as long as I've known him. If he made a mistake, it might have been for the right reasons. Or maybe it's forgivable. Or maybe, it wasn't a mistake at all. We don't know until we talk to him." He took her by the shoulders, trying to give her a certainty he didn't fully believe. "He gave you the clue. You figured it out. No matter what…we have to see this through. If only so you can have some answers."

"Answers. What possible answer could make this not awful?"

"I don't know. But that doesn't mean there isn't one."

She leaned into him. They didn't have the time, and yet he couldn't rush her. Not when she was grappling with what he knew too well was… He hated his father. Always had. Yet even with all that hate, it was complicated knowing he was related to someone so awful.

Duke wasn't awful. Grandma had that right. Whatever mistake he might have made, it wouldn't have been done out of cruelty. Tucker had to believe that, and with answers, they'd all be able to move forward.

"Come on. Let's head over to Bonesteel. We'll meet with Cody and come up with a plan to get to Duke. He wanted us to find this, Rach. Maybe it's useful. Important."

"Should we leave it with Grandma Pauline if it's so important?"

"She'll keep it safe. That's why it's here in the first place."

"Tucker..." She pulled away, and tilted her head toward him. Her eyebrows drew together and she opened her mouth but didn't say anything, as if she was struggling to come up with the words.

She needed reassurance, and Tucker didn't feel very sure, but he wanted to give that to her. Wanted her to be able to believe in Duke and trust that they were doing the right thing trying to save him from North Star, the Viannis *and* the Sons. "It'll be okay. I'm not saying it will be easy, but it'll be okay. I know it."

It had to be.

Chapter Seventeen

Tucker had to lead Rachel to Cody and Nina's door. Rachel had been to their house in Bonesteel a few times, but most family get-togethers were at one of the ranches. She didn't know her way around very many other places.

Tucker had explained he was parking around back, so she knew she was being led to the back door, which opened into a kitchen. Since it was the middle of the day, Nina was probably teaching her seven-year-old Brianna and Liza's half sister, the just-turned-five Gigi. Her and Liza traded off homeschool-teaching duties.

The door squeaked open. Immediately Nina went, "Oh," as if she knew exactly what was going on.

Then Rachel was quickly being ushered inside and greeted by her enthusiastic niece.

"Aunt Rachel! I didn't know you were coming over. Are you good at adding?"

"Brianna," Nina said in that warning tone moms always seemed to have. "No having Rachel or Tuck do your math while I go get your father."

"Where's Gigi?" Rachel asked as she heard Nina retreat.

"She's sick. I heard Aunt Liza say she threw up *everywhere*," Brianna said with some glee. "If you had three hundred and twenty-four…um, apples. And then Uncle Tuck brought you fifty-seven more—"

"Brianna!" Nina yelled from somewhere deeper in the house.

Brianna humphed. "Why are you guys visiting in the middle of the day?" Brianna seemed to suddenly realize it was odd timing. "Is there trouble again?"

Poor girl. She was way too intimately acquainted with trouble. Rachel forced a reassuring smile. "Just a little, but it's a problem for Uncle Tuck and me. Nothing for you to worry about."

"You need Daddy's help?"

"Only for a few minutes," Tucker interjected. "He won't even have to leave home."

Brianna sighed with some relief. "So are you guys going to get married then?"

Tucker seemed to choke on his own spit, and Rachel found herself utterly speechless.

"What now?" Tuck finally managed, though his voice sounded croaky at best.

"Well, when Mommy and Daddy were in trouble, they ended up getting married. And same with Aunt Liza and Uncle Jamison. Then Uncle Gage and Aunt Felicity are getting married and having a baby. Uncle Brady and Aunt Cecilia aren't getting married yet, but I heard Mom say that it was *inevitable*. Now you two are in trouble. So…"

"No, sweetheart, that's not…how it works…exactly." Tucker sounded so pained it was almost funny.

There was the sound of footsteps and low murmurs. Then Nina's voice. "Get your math book, Bri. We'll go finish up in the living room."

There was a long suffering sigh and the shuffle of books, papers and feet.

"Say goodbye to your aunt and uncle."

"Aren't they going to stay for dinner? We could order pizza." Nina must have given her a significant mom look because Brianna groaned and stomped away.

Rachel felt Nina's slim hand on her arm. "I'm sure Cody and Tucker can take care of whatever this is."

Rachel slid her arm away. "Don't do that to me. You didn't let Cody and Jamison handle your thing."

"Rach, I'm just saying… You're not a part of this. You could go home and—"

"I *am* a part of this. I'm the only reason we've gotten this far. Isn't that right, Tucker?"

There was a hesitation, like he might refute her so Nina could whisk her away and keep her safe. But there was no safety here. Whether she helped get Dad away from North Star or these other groups or not, Dad had still lied to her—to all of them.

She wanted to believe there was a reason for it. Maybe she had to do this so she could actually…see it. If someone just told her, even Dad, that it was for her own good…

She'd never be able to forgive him.

"Rachel's right," Tucker finally said. "We wouldn't be this far without her. If we're going to get Duke away from North Star—"

"Woah, woah, woah," Cody's voice interrupted Tucker. "What makes you think you're getting *anyone* away from North Star?"

"They tried to kidnap me," Rachel said.

"Rach, if they tried, you'd be kidnapped."

"No, she's right," Tucker told him. "They sent this woman named Shay to take her. They must have been listening in somehow and knew she was getting clues about everything from her dreams. Shay and I fought—"

"No offense, Tuck, but Shay'd take you down in a heartbeat."

"You know her that well?"

There was a pause. "I worked with her quite a bit. She's helped me out of a few jams."

"I have to go help Bri," Nina said softly. "Just…be careful. Both of you." Rachel felt arms wrap around her and squeeze, then heard the sounds of Nina exiting the room.

"I pointed out to Shay that kidnapping an innocent bystander wasn't necessary," Tucker said. "That I wouldn't let anyone put a mission above her life. Eventually, she agreed with me."

"So, she let you go."

"Yeah. Because she knew I was right. She knew that what North Star has been doing isn't what I signed up for."

"What *you* signed up for?"

Tucker huffed out a breath. "What? You don't believe they'd tap me for some help? I'm not North Star material?"

"I didn't say that," Cody said evenly.

Rachel wanted to defend Tucker, but it wouldn't change the fact he felt slighted by his baby brother. Still, she understood a little too well what it was like to be overlooked. Underestimated. To not fully realize it until the crap hit the fan.

I'm sure Cody and Tucker can take care of whatever this is. Nina meant well, because she loved her. Because they were sisters. But it still hurt.

Silence remained. Tucker and Cody were likely having some nonverbal conversation she'd never be privy to.

Rachel could be mad about that, and pout, or she could take matters into her own hands. "After we ran from Shay, after she let us, Dad sent us a note, through Shay. It led us to the weapon that did this to me." She pointed at her face. "We could hand that over to North Star, but what would they do with it?"

Cody didn't answer for a few seconds. "I couldn't say."

"But you know as well as I do that it wouldn't be used to save my dad or keep me safe. It would be used to take someone down."

"Taking those people down *would* be keeping you safe."

"Would it? Because Ace is in jail. So is Elijah and Andy Jay and all the Sons members who've come after you all this year. They're all in *jail*. Am I safe, Cody? Are you?"

Cody didn't have anything to say to that, either.

"Dad sent me this note in secret. He wanted me to get that evidence without North Star knowing. What does that tell you about what North Star is doing? Shay let us go and she *works* for North Star."

"Look, you avoided getting kidnapped because Shay let you. Maybe you're right and North Star can get a little…people blind. Regardless, you can't get into North Star and get Duke out. You just can't. They're too well organized."

"You know where he's being held?" Tucker asked.

"I have an idea. You wouldn't make it within fifty yards without them picking you up. Then they'd have Rachel like they wanted in the first place. And you're right, mission comes first. It has to or they can't do what they do."

"I don't care what they do, Cody. I care about my father. I care about the fact someone did this to me when I was *three*, and I won't let them do anything else to my family. Maybe I'm not a detective or a secret operative, but I sure as hell am in the middle of this thing."

"She's right," Tucker said softly. "She remembers things. She knows Duke. North Star wanted to kidnap her. She's smack dab in the middle of this."

"Why are you, Tuck?"

"Because North Star asked me to be. But they've taken a wrong turn, and I won't let that hurt Duke.

They asked me to keep his daughters safe—so that's what I'm going to do."

"If I tell you where Duke probably is, like I said, it's not going to go well. I can't tell you how to sneak in. They'll know you're coming a mile away. I can't help you get in there. I'm not part of North Star anymore, and as much as I know, they know I know it. They'd have protections against it if they wanted to keep me—or someone related to me—out."

"You know how to get in touch with Shay."

When Cody spoke, his voice was firm. "I won't get her kicked out."

"She didn't sound like she was in it for the long run," Rachel said. "She got us the note. Surely you can get in touch with her and give her the option of helping us."

"That won't be necessary."

It was a woman's voice, and Rachel could only assume it was Shay herself.

"So, you'll help us?" Rachel demanded.

"Yeah, but you're not going to like how."

TUCKER HAD TO blink to make sure that was indeed Shay entering the room from where Nina and Brianna had disappeared earlier. "How…"

"I figured you'd hit up Cody once you figured out Duke's note. The weapon that did that, huh?" Shay said, nodding toward Rachel's face.

Tucker glared at Cody. "You didn't tell me she was there," he gritted out.

"He didn't know," Shay said with a grin. "Nina's the one who gave me the heads-up."

"I never should have let you two become friends," Cody muttered. "You'll get kicked out. This would be the last straw."

"I've been saying that for months now. Apparently, Granger loves me. Also, you didn't *let* me become friends with your wife."

"What aren't we going to like?" Tucker demanded, wanting to keep the focus on what needed to be done.

"My brother do that?" Cody asked with some surprise as he noticed Shay's bruised cheek.

Shay shook her head. "He wouldn't hit a woman," she said as if that was a *bad* thing. "Rachel did it."

Cody let out a low whistle. "Nice work, Rach."

"Can we focus?" Tucker demanded.

"So, all you Wyatts are wound that tight, eh?" Shay said to Cody, earning a frown from both Wyatts in question. "Duke's not going to talk to me. Even if I said I was in cahoots with you. Why do you think that letter I smuggled out was in code? We need to get Rachel to him."

"Or we need to get Duke to Rachel."

Shay shook her head. She was still dressed all in black, but no mask or hat. Her blond hair was pulled back in a tight ponytail and she stood there, legs spread, arms folded across her chest like some kind of special ops soldier.

In a way, Tucker supposed she was.

"We're not getting Duke out of there. It's not possible unless they're distracted by something they need more than Duke's knowledge of the Viannis and the Sons." Shay looked meaningfully at Rachel.

Even though it didn't change what she'd said, Tucker moved in between Shay and Rachel. "No."

"Don't say no," Rachel told him. "Not *for* me. You'll tell me what you mean, and *I'll* say no if I see fit."

"She wants to use you as bait," Tucker said disgustedly.

"And what's wrong with that?" Rachel returned.

He, of course, couldn't answer that. What he thought was wrong with that wouldn't be appreciated.

"How would we do it?" Rachel asked calmly.

Tucker didn't know how she could be calm. Maybe because she hadn't actually seen that knife that had been used to take away her eyesight, sitting there grotesquely in a box. Maybe because she didn't fully grasp what the Sons could do on their own, let alone with another dangerous group of criminals.

Or maybe she was calm because she lived that night over and over again in her dreams and she had no control over that. This…she felt like she could act on.

How could he not support that?

"I take you to headquarters," Shay began. "I'll say I tracked you down and convinced you to ditch Tucker. You'll say you want to help your father in whatever way you can. Which is all true."

"Except it's sending her into the lion's den."

"Only one, and the less dangerous of the three," Shay returned. "While they're focused on getting information from Rachel, it'll give me a chance to slip out and grab Tucker. We'll work together to get Duke out."

"Except Rachel is stuck in there then."

"It might not matter," Rachel said. "Depending on what the full truth is."

"No, it'll matter," Shay corrected. "The whole point of me going against the group I've dedicated six years of my life to is to help keep you and your father from being caught in a crossfire that's got nothing to do with you, and only a little to do with your father. Tucker will take Duke. I'll go back in and get Rachel."

"It'll be your last hurrah. You take people out of North Star custody, no amount of Granger liking you keeps you in North Star," Cody said gravely.

"I'm okay with that. I wasn't at first. But this whole thing… It's been different since you left, Cody. Since Ace has been in jail. It should have made it easier, but we're going at it harder and caring less and less who gets caught in the middle. I won't be party to it any longer."

"All right, what do you need from me?" Cody asked.

Cody and Shay discussed some technical stuff to do with the North Star security systems and Tucker turned to Rachel. She had her chin set stubbornly. It was stupid to try to convince her to back out of this, but…

"You're risking your life. I want you to understand that."

"Duke already risked it," Rachel replied. "Risked Sarah and me, all of us. Didn't he? By going with them."

"North Star brought me in because he wanted you protected. I was there to make sure you weren't brought into the thick of things."

"Maybe, but we're here. In the thick of things. I won't be swept into a corner. Maybe what we found in the safe hurts my feelings. It…hurts. Even if my father has a good reason, to know that's there is painful. But you were the one who told me it doesn't change the fact he's a good man who's always been a good father. He loved my mother. He loved me and my sisters. He raised us when she died, and all the while…" She blew out a breath. "You've all lived with terrible things. Now, I'm living with mine. I won't back down. You wouldn't. None of my sisters would. None of your brothers would, and I know my father wouldn't. So. Why should you expect me to?"

"It's not that I expect you to, Rach. It's that I care about you and I want you to be safe." Which he would have said before kissing her. Of course, he cared about her—about all the Knights. But it felt heavier in his chest, even in this kitchen with his brother and a North Star operative a few feet away.

She reached out and he took her hand. She squeezed it and smiled at him. "We're all doing this because we care about each other."

Which wasn't exactly what he'd meant or felt. He'd meant *her* in a very uncomfortably specific way.

"It's a risk, but it's not like I'm walking into Sons territory. I'm walking into a group who wants to take down two very bad groups of people. It's the lowest risk I could take. You're taking a bigger one trying to get Dad out." Her hand slid up his arm, shoulder, until her palm cupped his cheek. "So, we both have to support each other taking risks to end all this danger. I'd like to have my life back. I'm sorry I ever wanted something different. It was perfectly nice. Well, mostly." Her thumb moved across his jaw, then she dropped her hand as if she remembered there were other people in the room.

"We should move immediately, right?" she asked.

"Right," Shay agreed. She gave Tucker a considering look but crossed to Rachel. "I'm going to give you a panic button of sorts. It's tiny and easy to lose, so I'm going to sew it into the sleeve of your shirt. Okay?"

Rachel nodded and held out her arm to Shay. Shay worked on sewing the tiny button into the inside of Rachel's sleeve, and Tucker was not at all surprised his brother pulled him away from Rachel and into the hallway.

"It's not really going to go down like this."

"What isn't?" Tucker muttered.

"You and Rachel? Don't think I didn't notice that little moment. That's five for five."

Tucker shrugged uncomfortably. "It's not like that…exactly."

"Yeah, *exactly*." Then Cody laughed. Loud and hard. "Jesus. Dev and Sarah."

"Not in a million years," Tucker said, managing a small laugh of his own. "They'd eat each other alive first."

Cody shook his head. "Don't bet against it."

Chapter Eighteen

Rachel did her best not to act nervous. She knew Tucker didn't approve of this plan, but he was going through with it because of her.

So she had to be brave. She had to be sure. Too bad she was wholly terrified.

Shay had sewn a *panic button* into her shirt, instructing her that it had to be pressed three times to send a signal. Which would go to Cody, who would no doubt send the whole Wyatt clan after her.

After *her*, because she was going to be the distraction. The bait. She was going to walk into North Star and demand to see her father.

Shay warned her they wouldn't let that happen. That they'd likely put her in an interrogation room, holding the carrot of seeing her father over her head until she answered all their questions.

She was supposed to refuse. Give them bits and pieces to keep their attention, but mostly be difficult, and lie if necessary. So that all eyes were on her while Shay and Tucker snuck in to get Duke out.

It was a lot of pressure, and while her family

treated her as an equal more often than not, no one had actually ever put *pressure* on her. The hardest thing she'd ever done up to this point was demand to teach art classes at the rez. There had been some pressure to succeed so no one pitied her for failing, but not like this.

"Okay, you'll drop us here," Shay instructed Tucker.

The car came to a halt. Rachel was seated in the back. She hadn't realized until this moment she was going to have to trust Shay implicitly, not just to be telling the truth but to guide her through a completely unknown setting.

When the door next to her opened, Rachel had to fight the desire to lean away. To refuse to get out. She stepped into the autumn afternoon instead.

"Don't be afraid to speak up if I'm walking too fast or something. Better to get there in one piece than worry about hurting my feelings or whatever."

The no-nonsense way Shay took her arm and said those words had Rachel's shoulders relaxing. Maybe it was scary, but at least Shay wasn't going to be all weird about her being blind.

"Let me talk to her for a minute," Tucker said briskly.

"All right," Shay said. She let Rachel's arm go and Tuck's hands closed over her shoulders. He gave them a squeeze.

"You be smart. Take care of yourself first. I couldn't…" He let out a ragged breath. "I don't want you hurt, Rach."

"Tuck…" She didn't know what to say. There wasn't time to say anything. So, she could only give him what he'd given her. "I don't want you hurt, either."

"Then we'll stick to the plan, and everything will be okay."

"You don't actually believe that," she said, both because she didn't and because she could hear it in his voice that he didn't, either. "We'll stick to the plan, and hope for the best. And if the best blows up in our face, we'll just have to fight like hell."

He chuckled softly. "Yeah, you got that right."

Then, before she could say anything else, he kissed her. It wasn't sweet or light. It was firm, a little fierce and had her heart beating for an entirely new reason aside from fear. "Stay safe, Rach."

He released her, and she was passed off to Shay. It was disorienting for a lot of reasons, but the whole being shuttled between people in foreign settings certainly undercut the happy buzz of that kiss.

"They all like that?" Shay asked, leading her forward.

"Like what?"

"Like…gentlemen, but not wimps about it. Think of women as equals, and aren't too keen on using them as a punching bag. Kiss like that and then walk away to save your butt—while you're also busy saving your own butt."

Rachel had to smile. "Pretty much."

Shay didn't say anything else to that, just kept leading Rachel forward.

"Can you describe it to me? Give me some kind of idea of where they're going to take me and how to get out?"

"Good idea." Shay explained that it looked like a hunting cabin from the outside. Inside, they had different holding rooms, a medical center and a tech center. She explained the layout, which room Duke was in and what room they'd probably take her into.

"So, if for whatever reason you want to run, they're going to be able to track you until you get off the property. Not much use in it. But, to get out the door, you'd just need to remember how to get to the hallway."

Rachel filed all that away, tried to bring her own picture to her mind. It would help if she found herself needing to escape.

Shay brought her to a stop. "All right. Here we go."

Rachel expected her to knock or buzz in or something, but the sound of the door opening was the first thing she heard once they stopped.

"This is an interesting turn of events," a male voice said. "Where's the guard dog who gave you that shiner?"

"I got to her without Wyatt," Shay returned. She spoke differently to the man. Sharp. All business. Any hint of the woman who'd asked if the Wyatts were all like that was gone.

"How?"

"Everyone has to take a bathroom break now and again, Parker. Now are you going to step aside or what?"

The man grumbled, but Rachel was being led forward so he'd clearly allowed entrance. "Wait here for McMillan."

Rachel listened as the footsteps quieted.

"McMillan is my supervisor," Shay said in a whisper. "He's all bark and mostly no bite. I imagine since he's been handling Duke, he's going to be the one who questions you. If not? Be as difficult as possible until they bring McMillan in."

"All right."

"Shay."

Rachel had assumed Shay was the woman's first name all this time. But the way her superior barked it out, Rachel had to wonder if it was actually her last name.

"Sir. A little late, but better late than never."

"How'd you manage what you failed at earlier?" He emphasized the word fail as though failure was the absolute worst thing a person could do.

"Followed them. They were on the run, off their home territory. Wyatt let his guard down and I convinced Rachel to talk to us. She's willing, if you let her see her father."

"Dymon!" the man yelled.

More footsteps, a few hushed words, then someone took her other arm. Shay's grip tightened and Rachel felt a bit like she was in the middle of a tug-of-war.

"Who's that?" Shay asked, suspicion threading through her voice.

"Your replacement," McMillan said, his voice so

chilly Rachel thought to shiver. "Shay. You're done here."

"Sir, I think a woman should—"

"I said you're done here," McMillan said, and this was no bark or yell. It was cold, a succinct *or-else* order.

Shay slowly released her arm, and Rachel was being led away. The grip on her other arm was unnecessarily rough. She remembered what Shay said about being difficult. "You're hurting me," she said, trying to tug her arm away from the too-tight grasp.

"Oh, you have no idea what's in store for you, little girl," the voice hissed.

Rachel's entire body went cold. She recognized that voice.

It was the voice from her dream.

"Something isn't right."

Tucker whirled, gun in hand. It was only Shay, but she'd snuck up on him soundlessly. Still, he didn't have time to worry about that. "*What* isn't right?"

"New guy. McMillan isn't in the habit of hiring new guys."

"He hired me."

"Not the same. You're not an operative. You're like a…liaison. This guy I've *never seen* is in the South Dakota headquarters of North Star, and I've never heard his name or even heard whispers of a new guy." She rubbed a hand over the back of her neck. "Something isn't right."

"You left Rachel in there? When something wasn't right?"

"Calm down," Shay said sharply. She pulled her phone to her ear. "Wyatt? Yeah, I need you to do some spying for me." She sighed heavily. "Yeah, yeah, yeah, you ask your wife if she thinks you should stay out of it when her sister is in North Star headquarters with a stranger." Another pause. "Yup, that's what I thought. Someone named Dymon. Get me anything you've got on him." She hung up, shoved her phone in her pocket.

"Are you sure they're not tracking you through that?" he asked.

"Do you think I'm dumb? I had your brother take care of all the tracking devices when we were there."

"It never occurred to you that a group that tracked your every move might not be on the up and up?"

"Look. You don't know anything about North Star, or McMillan for that matter," she snapped. "Like that your father was responsible for his wife's death."

Tucker didn't say anything because he hadn't known that. At all.

"Grief does funny things to people. He's not a bad guy, and whatever is going on doesn't make him one. It makes him…human. And, hell, aren't we all?"

Tucker didn't want to think about how human they all were. Not when being human meant making mistakes, and they couldn't make any with Rachel inside North Star.

"Let's move. The less time she has to be in there, the better."

Shay nodded. "On that, we can agree."

It was Shay's plan since she knew the headquarters—what from the outside looked like an upscale hunting cabin. They bypassed the front, and Shay would occasionally pause to do something on her phone that allegedly moved the cameras or turned off security or whatever else North Star had in place.

"You sure you know all of those?"

"I installed them. I sure as hell should." They finally got to the back door, which was next to a garage of sorts. "I'm going in. I imagine everyone knows I got the boot, but I've got stuff in there. So, I'm going in to collect my stuff. When no one's watching, I'll open this garage and the door inside. You'll head straight for it. If I don't have Duke waiting, you move back into the garage. Check at five-minute intervals. Once he's there, you sneak him out the garage, go in the direct route we came and get to the car. Once you're there, you'll give me fifteen minutes. If I don't show up with Rachel, you get Duke out. I'll contact you or your brother with the next step once I've got Rachel. And whatever you do, don't go all Wyatt on me."

"What does that mean?"

"Don't play the hero. You may hear or see something you don't like, but you focus on Duke. You're going to want to barge back in here and get Rachel, but I've got it handled. You trust me and I trust you."

"That's asking a lot."

"Yeah, it is," she agreed. "For both of us. You up for the challenge?"

He didn't want to be. Trusting someone he barely knew was like tossing a coin with Rachel's life on the line, but hadn't he already done that? Besides, Shay didn't strike him as a stupid woman and she was putting at least some of her safety in *his* hands. It was a risk they both had to take.

"How long do I wait until I open the door?"

"Minute the garage opens you're in. You hear a whistle—I don't mean a sharp whistle, I mean like me whistling a tune—you go back and hide in the garage. We'll keep trying till it's clear."

Tucker nodded. "All right."

Shay nodded in return, then she slid in the back door. Tucker stood in the corner next to the garage, doing his best to hide his body in the way Shay had instructed. When the garage door opened, almost soundlessly, he slipped inside. Then immediately located the door inside and headed for it.

He turned the knob, eased it open and himself inside. He was in a basement that bizarrely looked like any house's basement might. A TV room in a little finished alcove, a laundry area on the opposite side. The hallway was dark.

Tucker remembered what Shay had said and went back to the garage, waited the aforementioned five minutes, then went inside again. He kept his mind blank. Thought of it like detective work—often boring and tedious…until it wasn't.

Fifteen minutes had passed, and finally Duke appeared. Duke studied him there at the end of the hallway and didn't budge. That was when Tucker realized Shay was standing behind him, with a gun to his back, and he only moved forward toward Tuck when she poked it into his back again.

"He's being difficult," she hissed. "Fix it. I've got maybe ten minutes before Parker comes back. Maybe."

Fix Duke Knight's hard head? Yeah, in what world? Still, Tucker moved forward. "We have to get you out."

"Why should I trust you? I trusted Granger and look what happened. Now I've got two North Star operatives trying to sneak me out? That smells like a setup, boy."

"We're trying to help you. It's because of *you*, and what they want to do with your family, that we're turning our back on North Star."

Duke didn't respond to that. "Who's watching the girls?"

Tucker hesitated. "We're all doing what we should be doing," he said carefully, already knowing that wouldn't fly. His hesitation spoke volumes.

Duke narrowed his eyes. "You've always been a crap liar. Where's Rachel?"

"She's…" Tucker couldn't tell Duke under any circumstances. If he knew Rachel was upstairs, he'd charge up there like an angry bull.

"She's upstairs keeping them busy," Shay said.

Tucker nearly groaned, but he had to leap in front of Duke as he charged for the stairs. Though Tucker

was taller, Duke was thicker, and he'd been a cowboy for thirty some years so he was no slouch. Still,
Tucker had been trained to deal with threats bigger
than him.

Tucker managed to shove him a step back. "You
don't know what will happen to her or you if you
barge in there. Trust that we've got this under control."

"That's my daughter you're risking," Duke said,
and though his voice was ruthlessly controlled in
volume, his eyes bulged and the tendons in his neck
stood out like he was about to explode.

Tucker couldn't blame him if he did.

"She risked herself, buddy. For you. So maybe
you make it easy on us so I can get her out without
causing a storm where someone gets hurt," Shay said
with absolutely *no* finesse.

Which was apparently what Duke needed to hear.
He moved forward, though his scowl was still in
place. Tucker passed him up to get to the door first.
As he did, Duke he full-on sneered.

"I'm holding you personally responsible."

"As if I'm not," Tucker muttered. He glanced back
at Shay.

"Take him out, just like we said. I'll go get her."

Tucker nodded. He led Duke into the garage quietly. Then out. Tucker had to hope Shay remembered
to close it.

"Shay will bring Rachel to us," Tucker told him,
moving in the same direction they'd come. Shay had

disabled the cameras, but they could have come back on. Still, he had to trust she'd handle it.

"I can't believe you'd be this stupid," Duke muttered, though he followed behind Tucker.

Tucker looked over his shoulder and raised an eyebrow. "That's really how you want to play this? When we found the weapon that blinded your daughter in Grandma Pauline's safe? I had to beg your daughter to understand that you *must* have had a good reason for that. So—"

Tucker's phone vibrated. He shook his head and kept walking. When it vibrated again, he swore under his breath and pulled the phone out of his pocket. They were finally in some tree cover, but not to the car yet. Tucker saw it was Cody calling and answered.

"Cody—"

"Shay didn't answer, but this is important. I got into North Star's system to look up this Dymon guy. I managed a quick glimpse into the files before they figured out I was hacking in and kicked me right back out. This guy's got connections to Vianni. I suppose he could be a double agent—helping out North Star. Sort of like us."

"Except we never worked for the Sons or our father." Tucker thought about everything Shay had told him. About this whole lead up. "He's working for Vianni. They're so hung up on taking down the Sons, they don't care who they go to bed with."

"Maybe," Cody replied gravely. "Either way? I'd get Rachel out of there ASAP."

Chapter Nineteen

Fear paralyzed Rachel, but all the man from her nightmares had done was drag her deeper into the building and then shove her into a chair. He was almost immediately followed by someone else, and once that person spoke, she knew it was the head guy. What had Shay called him? McMillan?

At least she wasn't alone with her nightmare—but would this man be just as bad?

It didn't matter. As long as she was in this building, she had a chance of survival. Dad was here. Shay was here. Tuck was here. She would survive.

Rachel studied what she could of the room. She reached out and felt the table in front of her. So she was sitting on an uncomfortable chair at a table. The man across from her was McMillan. He had a big dark presence and he appeared to move in such a way that she figured it meant he was sitting down at the table, too. The other man was dressed all in dark colors, too, but not as broad as McMillan. Not as...still.

She remembered that about him from her dream. A need to move. He stood next to McMillan, a vibrating presence. In the vague way she saw things, they appeared to be a unit.

Did McMillan know? Was North Star actually in bed with Vianni? It was a horrible thought. If they were, she was dead. Shay and Tucker were likely dead, too, and God knew her father was already dead.

Except he wasn't. They'd gone to rescue him. So, surely North Star didn't know.

Unless they needed that knife, and that was the only reason her father was still alive.

Rachel swallowed. "I just want to see my father," she said through a too-tight throat, terror making her feel like lead all the way through. But she couldn't just lie down and die.

She had to figure out a way to fight.

"That's understandable, Ms. Knight. Your father is here under our protection. Just how much do you know about that?"

She didn't let her eyes drift to the man standing. He had to know she knew who he was. Didn't he? Or would he assume because she was blind that she didn't? But he had to have felt how afraid she was. Her reaction to his voice.

He had to know she knew.

"Miss?"

Rachel sucked in an audible breath. McMillan had asked her a question. "I'm sorry. I… I don't know. I know Shay tried to kidnap me at the ranch. She and Tucker fought and Tucker got me away from her. She followed us, I guess. She…" Rachel had never been a good liar, but she let the genuine fear she felt consume her. Her voice shook. She shook. They'd believe it was a result of fear of the situation, not her lies. "She found me later. While Tucker was... Anyway, she said I could see and talk to my father if I came with her. That everything would be explained if I came with her."

"Our operative was sent to retrieve you because of the dream you've been having. Can you tell us about that?"

"I..." Rachel trailed off. They likely knew everything at this point. God knew the man from her nightmare did. If they'd been listening to Tucker before Shay's arrival, they had the full account of how her dream had morphed.

"It was just a nightmare. Just a...memory of what happened to me." She gestured at her face. "I don't see what it has to do with anything."

"You never dream past the moment you were hurt?" McMillan asked.

He made it all sound so clinical, but he couldn't see the nightmare, the reality in his mind like she could. "I was three. A madman slashed my face up and I was saved by a dog. What more would I know than that?"

"What about the knife?" It was the other man's voice. The voice from that dream, and she couldn't help but flinch at it.

"What knife?" she managed to whisper.

"Dymon." It was a warning from the man. "You're

not involved in the questioning. If you can't remember that, you can step outside."

She could all but *feel* the tamped-down energy humming off the nightmare man. Still, he didn't say anything else.

But he wanted to know about the knife. The knife in Grandma Pauline's safe. One thing she knew for certain, she couldn't tell them about that.

"I don't know what you're talking about. I told you about my dream, now I want to see my father."

"What do you know about your father's past?"

"None of your business," Rachel snapped. She wouldn't play the cowering victim anymore. Not when she couldn't decide if the man in front of her was good or bad or some mix of the two. But, regardless, she didn't have to be nice to him.

"The group who's after your father has aligned themselves with the Sons. You've got quite a few in-laws who are former Sons members, don't you?"

"If you think being held in that gang as a child against your will is being a *former member*, you're a monster."

The man sighed, like a disappointed teacher or parent.

"Miss, it'd be easier on you if you simply answer our questions. Once you tell us the truth, we'll take you to your father. I understand you're not part of this, but Duke Knight is in a very dangerous situation. He's trying to protect you, but it's not getting us anywhere. It seems this knife might be the answer to some of our…*problems*. I'm sure you want to help him, don't you?"

She thought about what one of her more smart-mouthed sisters might say in this situation. She managed a sneer and did her best impersonation of Liza. "Go to hell."

She thought about laying her cards out on the table. Lifting her chin and saying, *Is that why you've got someone associated with the Viannis in this room with us? To protect him and help him?*

But her father had gone willingly with this group. Shay and Cody, both people who'd helped her and other people, had worked for North Star believing in its mission. Tucker had helped them. Surely, they weren't evil. They couldn't be evil and fool so many good people.

But the Viannis and the Sons *were*. Didn't that mean someone could have infiltrated North Star without them knowing? Maybe North Star was smart, even good at helping people, but they hadn't brought down the Sons fully yet—and how long had it taken them to put Ace in jail?

They'd needed Jamison *and* Cody to do that. So it was plausible, especially by partnering with the Viannis who were more of an unknown, that the Viannis had in turn tricked North Star.

She wanted to believe that—needed to—because the alternative was too bleak to bear.

Rachel hitched in a breath. She had to find a way to tell the man across from her that the man standing beside him had been her would-be kidnapper—

the man who'd blinded her. But she couldn't write a note. And she couldn't just come out and *say* it either, because if the man across from her truly didn't know, he'd likely be killed, no matter what kind of operative he was.

"Why don't I go get you some water? Give you some time to think about what direction you want to go in. Dymon here will watch you until you're ready to talk."

It wasn't threatening exactly. Nor was it friendly. A mission. It was all about the mission.

She could hear his chair scrape back as if he was going to get to his feet. As if he was about to leave her with her nightmare. She reached forward in a desperate attempt to grab him. She managed to do just that, both her hands clasping McMillan's arm before he fully stood.

"Please, wait."

Cody had taught her Morse code when they'd been in middle school. She'd been feeling bad about something—she couldn't even remember what it was now. But he'd cheered her up by teaching her Morse code. They'd made a game of it that summer.

She didn't remember it all, and there wasn't time to stumble. Still, she had to try. She *had* to.

"Miss. Let go of my arm," McMillan said, not totally unkindly.

It gave her an awful hope, that glimmer of kindness.

So she tapped what she could think of, in the most succinct terms she could manage.

Danger.

My face.

Him.

He didn't say anything, but he also didn't pull his arm away. He didn't tell her to let go, so she tapped out the code again. The same code. The same words.

He withdrew his arm, but instead of getting up or doing something dismissive, he laid his hand on top of hers and gave it a reassuring pat. "All right," he said, his voice low and controlled. "Dymon, why don't you go get the water? I'll stay here with Ms. Knight."

"I'm sure you've got better things to do, boss."

"You're still new. I wouldn't push your luck," McMillan warned.

"I did pass all your tests. You hired me. You have to trust me to do this stuff when you've got more important things to do."

Rachel held her breath, but the one thing that steadied her the most was McMillan's hand over hers. A reassuring weight that he'd gotten her message, and wasn't going to leave her alone with this man.

"You told me you hadn't had any personal experience with the Knights," McMillan said quietly. "That you were too low on the Vianni totem pole to know more than a few stories about Curtis Washington and his new life in South Dakota."

"That's right," the nightmare man agreed.

"Is that the story you want to stick to right here and right now?"

There was a long tense silence. McMillan's hand

was still atop hers, and he began to tap. It took Rachel the second time through to figure it out.

Duck.

And then a gunshot went off.

There was a scuffle, a moan and then Rachel's arm was jerked as she was pulled out from under the table. "Wrong move, little girl."

Her nightmare had her again.

But this time—she would fight.

TUCKER SLID THE phone back into his pocket. He had to remain calm, because Duke was there and Duke wouldn't remain any kind of calm.

They had to head back to the house and get Rachel the hell out of there, even if he had to fight the entirety of North Star to do it.

"How familiar are you with the area?" Tucker asked, careful to keep his voice calm.

"Who was that on the phone?"

"I need you to get to the car. It's parked—"

"Oh, hell no," Duke snarled. "If you're going back in for my daughter, I'm going with you."

"We can't go in guns blazing. We can't—"

"I was a cop before you were born. I know a thing or two about what needs to be done, and I know what I'd do to keep my daughter safe."

At the end of his rope with indecision, Tucker snapped. "Like when a man tried to kidnap her and blinded her in the process?"

"He would have killed her," Duke said flatly. "But she's alive, because of me. She was hurt because of me, I get it. I don't know how to go back and change my life. I did what I thought was right, always. You perfect?"

No, he couldn't pretend to be that.

"Now, you got another one of those?" Duke asked, nodding at the gun in his hand.

"No." Tucker considered giving it to Duke. Tucker could fight better with his hands than Duke would be able to. It would—

The muffled echo of a *crack* interrupted the picturesque quiet. *Gunshot.* Tucker was off running before he'd even thought it through. He looked back at Duke once. He was running, too, but at a much slower pace.

"Go!" Duke shouted.

Which was all the encouragement Tucker needed to run at full speed back to the house. He'd break down the front door if he had to. He'd—

The explosion was so loud and powerful, it knocked Tucker back. He managed to stay on his feet, but for a horrible second he watched the entire house go up in flames as the sound of glass shattering and debris thundering surrounded him.

Then, after that split second, he ran toward it. What other option was there? People were inside. Rachel. Shay. But as he headed for the door, flames and smoke already enshrouding it, people came pouring out.

Tucker didn't see Shay. He didn't know if that was good or bad. The people were bloody, burned, coughing. He tried to find someone who looked remotely communicative, but they were all in various shapes of injury and couldn't answer his demands as the fire roared around them.

Two figures emerged then, one dragging the other. It was Shay. He couldn't tell whom she was dragging, but it wasn't Rachel. It was a large man. Tucker ran to her.

"Sorry," she rasped. She let go of the man she'd been hauling as people rushed forward to help him.

"He'd been shot," Shay rasped. "I went to the questioning room and he'd been shot. I couldn't find Rachel or the new guy. The Dymon guy. He had to have taken her out the back." She swayed but Tucker managed to catch her before she fell in a heap. "The explosion went off before I managed to do anything. Got emergency services coming," she continued as Tucker helped her into a sitting position on the ground. "But I don't think I'm going to be much help with Rachel."

"Give me your gun," Tucker managed, though terror pounded through him. When she did, he handed it to Duke who huffed up to them. "Shay thinks Rachel got out—or was taken out with someone. I'm going to find the trail. You do the same," he instructed to Duke.

Much as it pained him to leave this misery in his wake, he had to find Rachel before she met a worse fate. He had to make a wide circle around the flames to get to the back. He didn't worry about how close Duke was. He only worried about getting to Rachel.

Debris had flown more back here, which made

Tucker think the explosives had been detonated from the back. If whoever had Rachel had detonated the explosives by hand rather than remotely, it made sense. He'd have dragged Rachel out, then set off the bomb before he dragged her away.

Why drag her away and keep her alive, though? Why not let her die in the explosion?

But the guy hadn't. He'd taken her away, and regardless of the reason, Tucker had to believe that's what happened. Believe it and save her from this.

The yard was wooded. Tucker ruthlessly tamped down the panic gripping him. He had to think like a cop. Like the person he'd trained to be. Like his brothers. Calm in the face of crisis. In the face of someone he loved being taken.

He moved to the trees, looking for signs of tracks or struggle. There was nothing, but this was the only way the man could have gone. Tucker scoured the ground. He heard Duke's approach, though they didn't speak. They moved and they looked.

Tucker couldn't let himself think of Rachel being dragged out of that house by some Vianni thug. He couldn't think about the very real possibility that a Sons member was waiting to help—

"Wait." Tucker stopped. The rational thing to do was head for the trees and cover. Unless there was help waiting somewhere else. He tried to orient himself—the house—where it would be in relation to the Sons. The Sons current headquarters was a few hours away, *but* if they were meeting someone with a car, they'd need a road. It wouldn't have been the road

Shay had instructed him to use, because that was the main thoroughfare and would be too obvious.

"Go back to the house. Get a car. Anyone you can find," Tucker instructed, already moving north instead of his original west. "Once you've got a car, start driving for Flynn via Route 5. But be careful. The Sons might be involved."

With no time to spare, Tucker took off for Route 5. It meant running through open land, and that was dangerous, but if he could get to Rachel before they got her into a car, he didn't care what they did to him.

Chapter Twenty

Rachel slowly came to. Someone was dragging her, swearing. She could feel the ground beneath her, tell it was still daylight as the sun beat down on her face.

"Stupid plan," the man muttered.

It was like her dream. The fear and his muttering, but she was bigger. She was a woman now. She'd tried to fight him back in that room, but then everything had gone black.

Now, everything hurt, and her head pounded with excruciating pain. He must have knocked her out. She tried to kick out, but her ankles were tied together. So were her hands. She wanted to sob, but she knew instinctively if he didn't know she was awake, she was better off.

She wasn't going to be able to escape him with her hands and feet tied, and she couldn't use the button Shay had sewn into her sleeve. But she was alive. She supposed that was the silver lining. She wasn't dead.

At three years old, she'd survived being cut in the face and losing her sight. She could survive this. She *would* survive this.

The dragging stopped and he dropped her without warning. She couldn't hold back the sharp groan of pain.

"You awake?"

Dymon nudged her with his foot, and she kept her eyes closed. She let her head loll as she made another soft groaning noise, trying to pretend she was still unconscious. Or just coming to.

He muttered something. There was shuffling, the methodical plodding of feet like he was pacing the hard ground beneath them. "I need help. You can't expect me to make it all the way to the road. Yeah, yeah, yeah. Had to shoot McMillan. No, I didn't check. I had to get her out. Yeah, I know no casualties but things went sideways."

Rachel realized he was on the phone, talking to someone about getting her to the road. And if he got her to the road, she'd be put into a car. There'd be more people.

How would anyone find her if she was in a car? Wasn't there something about not ever letting anyone take you to a second location? Better to be killed than make it to that second location.

She swallowed down the fear. Somehow, someway, she had to fight. There was no waiting for Tucker or Shay to find her if there was a car waiting. Once she got in that car, she was as good as dead.

Dymon continued to grumble, and she slowly realized he was done with his phone conversation and was instead just talking to himself. Nothing important or telling, just complaints about being the only one with the balls to do the dirty work.

Rachel continued to pretend as though she were unconscious as she tried to figure out how on earth she was going to get out of this. She couldn't get out of the bonds on her wrists and ankles—they were too tight—but there had to be *something* she could do.

Back in the room, this man had wanted to know about her dream. About the knife. So…maybe she had to give that to him to keep him occupied, to buy herself time.

Hopefully enough time for Tucker to intercept her before the man got her to the car waiting for him.

She groaned some more, started to move, thrashed a bit against her bonds for effect. She blinked her eyes open.

Dymon grunted. "Thought I knocked you out better than that." He sighed heavily. "Guess I'll have to do a better job this time. Maybe just fix the problem altogether."

He was going to kill her. Here and now. No getting to the road. No second location, just death.

"No. No. Please—please don't." She swallowed at the fear and the bile rising in her throat. She had to be braver than this. "I know where it is," she blurted out. He'd mentioned the knife. She knew which one he was referring to. "I know who you are. I know what you did. And most importantly, I know where the knife you want is."

"So does your father."

"But you have me. Not him."

Dymon made a dismissive noise, and Rachel didn't know if it was agreement or refusal. She had no idea what he planned to do. He was simply a shadowy figure above her and she had no means to fight.

But no matter what was against her, she did not have to die without *trying* to survive. She knew what side of her the man was standing on, and she knew she was on a little bit of an incline. She could roll. And scream. Maybe someone would be able to save her.

If not? At least she'd tried.

She tested the incline, the placement of her own body and rocked back and forth a little. If he noticed, he didn't say anything. She counted inwardly and then did her best to use momentum to move into a roll—screaming as loud as she could while she started to gain speed down the incline.

Dymon swore at her viciously, and there was the sound of hard footsteps and a stumble and more swearing. Then her rolling was stopped as she knocked into what she was assuming was him.

"You idiot," he yelled.

She had the impression of him getting ready to strike. She could only brace for impact, but instead of pain—a new voice yelled.

"Don't move."

Rachel almost cried out at the sound of Tucker's voice, but the sound caught in her throat as cold steel was pressed to her forehead.

She didn't know where he was, or if he could see

her. She only knew there was a gun pressed to her head. She tried to see. Willed her eyes to work.

She could make out Dymon crouched above her, the gun pressed to her forehead. If she kicked out... He might shoot, but he might fall instead. They *were* on a hill. She just needed to place the kick in the right spot. Somehow.

"Rachel," Tucker's voice was very calm, and closer than it had been. "Do you remember what I told you about fighting?"

"She can't fight," the man said disgustedly. "I'm going to put a bullet through her brain. Then yours. Drop the gun."

"She's the only one who knows where it is," Tucker said, his voice so calm and...lethal. She might have shivered in fear if he weren't the only one who could help her survive this. "The evidence you're after. She's the only one."

Rachel thought about what Tucker had said about fighting. He'd told her to always go for the crotch. She just needed to kick the man in the crotch. She could figure out that general area, as long as she could position her body accordingly, she could do it.

"Curtis knows where it's at. I could kill her and—"

"I'm sorry, Rach. I know I promised never to lie to you again. So I won't. Duke died in the explosion."

Rachel jerked. It was a physical pain, even as she worked through what he'd *actually* said. He'd never promised not to lie to her. In fact, he had promised the opposite. So, Tuck was lying now? He had to be.

He was supposed to get Dad out. There was no way Dad was dead. No way.

Please, God.

She didn't focus on the words. On what Dymon and Tucker continued to argue about. She focused on the shadowy outline of the man. Where best to kick. Her aim just had to be right.

Or she was dead. And so was Tucker.

TUCKER COULD SEE Rachel trying to figure out the angle. Slowly, he began to crouch, acting as if he were going to put his gun down. He held one hand up in mock surrender, slowly inching his gun closer and closer to the ground.

He needed Rachel to kick, just one kick even if it wasn't in line would push the guy back. The hill would help with momentum, the gun would go up and Tucker could get a shot off.

All as long as the other guy didn't pull that trigger first.

"That explosion shouldn't have killed anyone," the man finally said after a long tense silence.

Tucker had seen enough of the wreckage to understand where the explosives had detonated. So he had to lie and hope for the best. "Only if everyone was in the front of the house. The basement is another story, and I had a man in there getting Duke out. They're both dead."

He hoped the lies would give Rachel some comfort that Duke wasn't actually dead. That no one was.

Unless McMillan had died of his gunshot wound.

"What's the point of an explosion that doesn't kill anyone, anyway? And you clearly had an in with North Star. Why not take Duke and get what you're after?"

"I could have," the man agreed with a sickening sneer. "But that doesn't finish the job from twenty years ago, does it?"

"This does, though."

All three of them jerked at the sound of Duke's voice, but it didn't last long, since Duke immediately fired a shot that had the man falling to the ground. Lifeless.

"Dad?" Rachel asked tremulously.

Tucker was already halfway to her, but since Duke had come up from the direction of the road, he was closer. He was murmuring to Rachel and untying the bonds on her hands so Tucker took the ones on her feet.

"Dad." They wrapped their arms around each other, so Tucker gave them a moment by making sure the other man was dead.

Tucker couldn't find a pulse, but he still pulled the gun out of his hand and the knife out of his boot. They weren't out of the woods yet, even if they'd managed to end one threat.

"We have to get out of here," Tucker said reluctantly, since Rachel was still clinging to Duke. "I can't imagine he was working alone."

"He's not. He was talking to someone about dragging me to the car. Is everyone at North Star all right? He shot McMillan. I…" Her hands were shaking, but Duke took them in his. Rachel kept talking. "When Shay took me in, they had this guy. Dymon is his name. He… I recognized his voice, from my dream."

"*He's* the guy?" Tucker looked at Duke for confirmation, and got a slight nod.

Tucker swore. She'd been kidnapped twice by the same man.

"I had to tell McMillan. I didn't think he understood how dangerous he was. So I tapped Morse code into his palm. Then he…this Dymon guy, he shot McMillan. It was so close and McMillan has to be dead, doesn't he?" Rachel asked, trying to wipe at her face, wet with tears. Tucker crouched next to her and used the hem of his shirt to wipe the rest of them away and clean her up a bit. She gave him a small smile.

Tucker could feel Duke's disapproving gaze, but they didn't have time for *that*.

"Shay dragged him out. They were getting him medical attention. He might make it." Probably a bit overly optimistic, but Tucker was willing to give her that in this moment. She'd used Morse code and… God, she was a wonder, but they had to get out of here. "Is there a car down at the road?"

"Yes. Not too far. I didn't see anyone else." Duke helped Rachel to her feet. Tucker flanked her on the other side. The ground was hilly, uneven, and helping Rachel toward the road was no easy task. She stumbled a few times, but they both held her up.

Through the trees, Tucker could begin to make

out the road, but it wasn't as deserted as it should have been.

"Get down," Tucker hissed, pulling Rachel to the ground as he ducked for cover behind a swell of earth.

"What is it?" Rachel asked.

"Three men and another car aside from the one Duke drove." Tucker moved so he could get another glimpse. Two men were circling the car Duke had parked in the ditch, and one of them was on his phone. "I need a better look."

Rachel's grip on his arm tightened. "No. You're not going anywhere. Let's just head back to North Star. I know I was unconscious, but it can't be that far."

Tucker didn't want to tell her there wasn't much of North Star left, but more importantly he wanted the opportunity to capture these men who were clearly in on the explosion and kidnapping attempt. The last thing anyone needed was them roaming free—to come after Duke or Rachel again, or whatever else was in their plans.

"Just give me five minutes. Stay put right here." He tugged his arm out of Rachel's grasp and had to trust Duke to keep her there and quiet.

He moved in silence, using trees and rocks and swells of land as cover, until he was close enough to see the three men. Tuck could hear them talking, but couldn't make out what they were saying. He considered getting closer, but with Duke and Rachel not that far away, it wasn't worth the risk.

Knowing he had to get them out of harm's way first, he carefully climbed his way back toward Duke and Rachel.

"Just the three men, but definitely waiting for their guy here to show up with Rachel."

"Vianni," Duke said disgustedly.

"No, they aren't Vianni men. Those are Sons men."

"You recognize them?" Duke asked.

"Got files on all three. The one on the right got off on a rape case because of a technicality. The one in the middle is my suspect on a murder case, but I don't have anything beyond circumstantial evidence and the prosecutor won't issue a warrant. The third has been in and out of jail for dealing drugs, armed robbery, you name it."

"Gotta love the legal system," Duke muttered. "What do we do, then? Pick them off?"

Tucker shook his head. "Too risky. They've got three guys, and three more high-powered weapons than we've got. Even if I use that guy's gun." Tucker glanced at Rachel. She wouldn't agree to this plan, but he didn't feel right trying to make it behind her back either. "Take her back."

"I will not—"

Duke spoke right over her. "What are you going to do?"

"They're accessory to kidnapping, possibly that explosion. I can arrest them."

"On your own, boy? Three against one isn't the best odds."

Tucker pulled out his phone. "I'll even the odds, then."

Duke's expression went even more granite. "And which of your brothers' lives are you willing to risk?"

It was a jab, but somewhere between that explosion and here he'd figured out what he hadn't fully understood until this moment. Yeah, four of his brothers were in love with Duke's foster daughters. Three of them had kids or babies on the way to support and protect. They had lives, and they shouldn't be taking unnecessary risks.

But they had. Over and over again this summer. Why?

Because nothing was ever going to be truly *good* until the Sons were gone. Truly taken out. The more of them they arrested, the more they had a chance of someone giving that last piece of evidence that brought the entire group to its knees.

"All of them, Duke. All of them."

Chapter Twenty-One

"I will not be carted off while you do something dangerous," Rachel said. She was careful to keep her voice quiet like they were doing, but what she really wanted to do was yell.

Her father's grip was tight on her arm and she wanted to shake it off and rage at him for even *considering* the fact they would go off and leave Tucker to do this, other Wyatt boys or no.

"Give me a second," Tucker said, and then she was being passed off and it was so *infuriating* because she couldn't exactly walk away, could she? Not in this foreign territory she didn't know.

"Listen. I'm not going to do anything stupid. My brothers, law enforcement agents who can also arrest these guys, are going to come and be backup. Maybe get some information that helps us land an even bigger blow to the Sons. I have to do this, and I'm sorry, I can't do it with you here."

Emotion clogged her throat. To get this far and then be relegated to…dead weight. Swept off by her father.

"It isn't right. I didn't *do* anything," she said, feeling raw and cracked open. She *couldn't* do anything. She understood she was a liability in the here and now and it was an awful, awful feeling.

Tucker's hands cupped her cheeks. "Yeah, figuring out where the evidence was, punching Shay in the face, using *Morse* code to tell McMillan his double agent was really a double agent, getting abducted and dragged through the woods but being smart enough to stay alive—nothing at all."

It should have been patronizing, but instead it was soothing. Because Tucker sounded…awestruck. Not in an *oh-poor-little-Rachel-managed-to-do-something* way, but like she was strong and all that stuff had mattered.

And it had. What might have happened if she hadn't gotten the message to McMillan? Yes, he might not have been shot, but Dymon could have gotten away with a lot more, and done a lot more damage.

"The Vianni part of this is over. Now, it's the Sons part. Let your father take you back to North Star. You've contributed, and probably have the concussion to prove it. Now, it's my turn. Okay?"

It wasn't *okay*, but she understood he had to do this. For himself. For his brothers. She moved her hands to his on her face, then slid her palms down the length of his arms, over his shoulders and up to his face.

"Okay," she said, and then pressed her mouth to his. He stiffened, likely because her father was around, but she didn't care. Not when he was going off into danger, and she was letting him.

But he relaxed into it, kissing her back in a way that felt like some kind of promise. He pulled back, taking her hands off his face.

"Be safe, and don't do a thing until your brothers are here." The kiss had felt like a promise, but she needed the words. "Promise me."

There was a pause, and he squeezed her hands in his. "I promise. Now, let your Dad take you back to North Star. You've got a hell of a bump on your head. I'm completely unscathed."

But he wouldn't stay that way necessarily. Still, there was nothing she could do about that. She'd only be in his way if she tried to convince him to take her along. Rachel knew she'd achieved some important things throughout this whole mess. Now her role was to step back and let him take the next step.

Hadn't she been harping at him to take help from his brothers—no matter what they'd been through and what he wanted to protect them from? Now, she had to take her own advice. Let him get the help he needed.

It didn't make it easy, but it also didn't make her a failure.

"Be safe," she repeated, giving his hands another squeeze before letting him pass her back to her father.

It was hard walking away, but as her father led her, the adrenaline began to fade into something heavier. Her head ached. Her body hurt. She felt nauseous.

"I don't know what you think you're doing kissing that boy," Dad grumbled, once they'd put some distance between them and Tucker. "I hope it doesn't mean what I think it means."

If she'd had any energy, she might have smiled. She was still so relieved he was alive, she couldn't muster any anger toward him. "If all of your daughters end up with a Wyatt, is that really so bad?"

"It is when they have to be dragged through pain and danger to arrive at that conclusion."

She frowned. *Dragged?* "It's your fault I'm even here. That Tucker is even here. This all begins with you."

"If this is all my fault, then the Sons are all those boys' faults."

She opened her mouth to argue, because of course that wasn't true. So, maybe it was true it wasn't her father's fault the Viannis were after him. But... "You had that knife. The one that hurt me. You lied to me, and made me doubt myself."

He was quiet for a few seconds as they walked. She could smell the acrid tinge of smoke on the air and knew they were close to getting to North Star.

"I did what I thought was right at the time. I'm sorry it hurt you, baby. You'll never know... I wanted you all safe. I'd been at the ranch in WITSEC for almost eight years when they found me again. I'd built a life. A better life than the one I'd grown up in, a better life than I'd had on the force. I had your mother, and I had you and the other girls. I could have run, but I wasn't going to give up this life I loved for some lowlife crime group. I needed something stronger than WITSEC, and evidence seemed the best way to keep them gone. An insurance policy."

"So, you let him go?"

"I didn't have him. I had to get you to the hospital. I couldn't go after him. But I could collect what he left behind. I could use it as my own threat. And it worked."

"Until now. Why now?"

"That's why I went to Granger McMillan. When I got a few veiled threats earlier this month, I went to his father. He'd been in charge of WITSEC when they moved me and we'd become friends. He recommended his son's organization to help get to the bottom of it. Because as far as I knew, the Viannis were all dead or in prison. Granger started looking into it, and when he found some connections between the Vianni group and the Sons, he brought me in."

"Of your own volition," she said.

"More or less. I wanted to protect you girls. Getting out of the way seemed the only option. Besides, I had the evidence. I knew I could use it if I needed to, and I thought McMillan could help me get it into the right hands, but I had to be sure I could trust him. I wasn't sure. I'm still not sure."

"He got shot. By this Dymon man. I told him he was the man from my dreams, more or less. He was going to help, but Dymon shot him first."

"Not Dymon. Vianni. The man who blinded you was Vianni's son," Duke explained. "McMillan told me he'd hired a Vianni underling in the hopes he'd be a double agent. He named some low level thug I hadn't ever had contact with, and I didn't recognize him. He must have had plastic surgery, taken on this new identity, because he was supposed to be dead. I was told a hit had taken him out right after your attack. I figured it was because he'd failed. You recognizing his voice is the only reason I put two and two together."

"So, you killed the man who was after you?"

"Appears so. I'm not saying that will end the Vianni group, but the family I put behind bars is mostly dead. It should be over."

"Except Tucker is still out there, trying to take down the Sons."

"He's a Wyatt, Rachel. They can put on a good show, but they can't let it go. Not while the Sons still exist, not while Ace lives, even if he's in prison. You get wrapped up in a Wyatt, that's what you're getting wrapped up in."

He didn't say it like it was some failing, only like it was fact. Which, no doubt, it was.

"You couldn't let injustice go when you saw it. You wouldn't run away when that came back to haunt you." She inhaled. "I know you love them like sons, and I understand why you'd be protective of your daughters. But you gave us the example. Doesn't it make sense that we'd all see that in you, even if we didn't know the details, and admire it in others?"

Duke was quiet for a long while, though instead

of holding her arm he slid his arm around her shoulders and led her that way.

"I want that head of yours checked out," he said, planting a gentle kiss near the place her head hurt the worst.

"Because of Tucker or just in general?"

Duke chuckled. "Both."

Something inside of her eased. She was still scared, worried for Tucker and all the Wyatts. Worried for McMillan and if he'd survived the gunshot wound. But her father was safe and here with her. One arm of this whole complicated thing had been taken care of.

Now Tucker needed to take care of his, and come back to her in one piece.

TUCKER WAS INTENT on keeping his promise. There was just one little problem. The three men on the road weren't staying there. Apparently, they'd grown tired of waiting for the dead man.

Jamison and Cody were close enough that they'd be here in the next ten to twenty minutes, if they rushed, which they likely would. The other three were much farther away, and Brady and Dev were physically compromised in that group.

But Cody had messaged them all.

Tucker wouldn't hide from the men walking up the side of the hill. He'd promised Rachel he wouldn't do anything until his brothers were here, but he could hardly help it when two of the three men were coming for him—one staying behind and poking through the car Duke had left.

Still, Tucker remained still. He kept his gun ready, and he listened.

"These Vianni morons. Soft city idiots. I'm already tired of cleaning up their messes."

"You can't say no to that kind of cash, though. Not with everything falling apart. I've been thinking of heading to Chicago myself."

The other man offered an anatomically impossible alternative and they both chuckled good-naturedly.

Tucker might have been swayed by the fact they sounded like any two men shooting the breeze. But he had files on these guys and he knew what they were capable of. Monsters could walk and talk and laugh, but what they were willing to *do* was what made them monsters.

They were coming up on him. Whatever happened, his brothers were on their way.

"What a lazy SOB. Couldn't even drag her this far?"

"Oh, he got this far," Tucker said companionably.

They whirled on him, one with a gun and the other with a knife. The one Tucker knew from his files as Justin Hollie sneered.

"A Wyatt." He flipped the knife in his hand. "Your free pass is over. We don't have to worry about hurting Ace's kids anymore."

Which wasn't what Tucker had expected anyone to say, let alone so gleefully. "Oh, yeah? Why's that?"

The man snorted. "Guess you're the last to hear.

Ace is dead. No need to come after us anymore. He can't do crap." He spread his arms wide. "Now, I'm a reasonable guy. I let you go, you leave us alone."

"Jail isn't dead."

"He died in jail. Crossed the wrong guy." Hollie snapped his fingers. "Boom. Gone. I heard it was even on the news."

Tucker couldn't process that. It couldn't possibly be true. "I don't believe you."

He shrugged. "No skin off my nose. Just telling you there's no beef here anymore."

"Of course, if you want one, we can give you one," the other man said. Travis Clyne, Tucker was pretty sure. The rapist who'd gotten off because the prosecutor hadn't thought the case was tight enough.

Tucker pushed away the thought of his father being dead. It just wasn't possible Ace Wyatt, the black cloud over his entire life, had just been…killed in jail like a common criminal, instead of the evil incarnate that he was.

Because there were two men who'd done plenty of evil right in front of him. "It turns out I've got a beef with kidnapping, explosions, killing people." He turned his gaze from Hollie to Clyne. "Rape."

"Your funeral." Clyne lifted his gun, but before he'd even gotten close to aiming, a shot rang out. It didn't appear to hit anyone, but Cody and Jamison appeared on either side of the Sons members.

The one with the knife whirled out toward Jamison, but Tucker shot, causing Hollie to stumble with a scream of pain. Cody punched Clyne before he could get a shot off at Tucker.

The third man came charging up, likely hearing the commotion. He stopped abruptly when all three Wyatts pointed guns at him. Looking at his friends writhing on the ground, then the guns, the man dropped his own.

"On your knees," Tucker ordered.

"Here. Tie him up." Cody tossed him some zip ties.

"Jeez. Do you always have these on you?" Tucker asked, quickly putting them to use.

"Never leave home without them," Cody returned, using more to tie up the man he'd punched. Jamison was doing the same.

They all stood at the same time.

"Unscathed again," Cody said with the shake of a head. "You've got the touch, Tuck."

Tuck let out a breath, almost a laugh. "Yeah, I felt bad about that for a while. I don't think I do so much anymore."

"I'll call county to pick these guys up. They've already got some guys collecting evidence on the explosives," Jamison said.

"There's also the car down on the road."

Jamison nodded. He quickly called all the information in. When he hung up, Tucker knew he had to broach the topic he didn't really want to understand.

"They said Ace is dead."

Jamison and Cody exchanged a glance. "We heard that too. Gage was getting everything confirmed when you messaged. We told him to stay put, we had this."

"Do you think he actually listened?"

Jamison smiled wryly. "The county guys will pass it along if he started heading this way."

"Do you think it's true?"

Both brothers sobered. Cody shrugged helplessly, and Jamison ran a hand over his neck.

"I don't know what to think," Jamison said. "So, let's focus on the here and now. Waiting for some guys to cart these morons away. Making sure Duke and Rachel are really safe."

Tucker turned to Cody. "North Star is beat up pretty good."

He nodded grimly. "They're all getting transported to the hospital. Liza's got the girls so Nina could drive over and pick up Duke and Rachel."

"She needs a doctor."

"I'm sure Nina will see to it."

Tucker nodded, but the possibility that Ace was dead overshadowed everything. "If he's dead, that means…it's over."

"We're law enforcement, Tuck," Jamison said, ever the cop. "As long as they're out there hurting people, it isn't over."

"No… But he is. Ace existing, linking us to it. The emotional aspect. It's over." He rubbed at his chest. "He can't be the boogeyman if he's dead."

Cody nodded. "So, we'll hope he is. Dead just the way he deserved. Broken and in jail with absolutely no fanfare."

Tucker let that settle through him. It seemed impossible, but it *would* be fitting. No standoff. No showy end. Nothing that could be described as godlike or awe-inspiring to the wrong kind. Ace's worst nightmare. To have a boring death no one remembered.

Tucker smiled at his brothers. Yeah, that's what he'd hope for.

Epilogue

There was fanfare.

No one said they were celebrating Ace Wyatt's death. They were celebrating Duke being okay. They were celebrating Brady healing and Felicity finding out she was having a girl. They were celebrating life and joy.

But Rachel knew that at least some of that joy was in knowing the man who'd caused them such pain and fear was well and truly gone.

Grandma Pauline had made a feast fit for royalty. They'd shoved everyone around the table as they always did. Even Dev was smiling. It was the best dinner in Rachel's memory.

Dad was safe. Everyone was safe. The men Tucker and his brothers had arrested had even agreed to talk, which had led to more arrests and a complete federal raid on the Sons compound. They hadn't been eradicated, but they had been taken down quite a few pegs.

And Ace Wyatt was dead. All the Wyatt men seemed…lighter. A little out of sorts, but lighter.

After dinner, no one was quick to leave. Even Dad and Sarah who had ranch chores to see to lingered.

"Why don't you go on out to the porch," Grandma Pauline said quietly into her ear.

Rachel frowned. "Why?"

"Just go on now."

Confused, Rachel did as she was told, stepping out into the quickly cooling off night.

"Rach? You're not headed back on your own are you?"

Tucker. She should have known. He must have snuck out, and Grandma Pauline had sent her to find out why.

"No." She moved toward his voice. "What are you doing out here all by yourself?"

He was quiet for a moment. "I'm not sure. Everyone's so happy. I'm happy. But… It's weird. I don't know how to feel about… I'm happy for all of them. Happy Ace isn't a shadow on our lives anymore, but I always assumed there'd be some big standoff. And now he's just gone. I'm happy, but it's…complicated."

"I think that's fair. I think you get to have whatever feelings on the matter you need to."

"Yeah, I guess so."

His arm came around her shoulders, so she wrapped hers around his waist. She sighed and relaxed into him. A good man, with a good heart. "I'm glad you weren't hurt."

"It seems we all managed to make it through okay. McMillan's going to be released from the hospital tomorrow."

"And Shay didn't lose her job, according to Nina."

"So, all's well that ends well, I guess."

Rachel thought on that. "It's not an ending, though. It's just life. We endured some bad parts. Now, we get to enjoy some good parts."

"Good parts," he echoed. He wound a strand of her hair around her finger. "You know one good part we seemed to have missed? I've never taken you out."

"Taken me out. Like…a date?"

"Yeah, like a date."

She grinned. There hadn't been time to talk much about the things that had transpired between them on a personal level. She'd been nervous to bring it up. Unsure. But he was asking her on a date. "I guess you should probably do that."

"Tomorrow night?"

"I'll see if I can clear my schedule."

They stood in the quiet for a long while. It was a nice moment. A settling moment. He was an honorable man, who'd take her out on a date, and take things slow. But he'd take them seriously, too. She liked to think it was what they both needed after this horrible year.

She turned in his arms, wrapping hers around his neck. "You're a good man, Tucker Wyatt. You're all good men. Whether Ace is dead or alive. That's always been true. Whether you got hurt fighting him or managed to escape unscathed. Who you are doesn't change. I hope you know that."

"I'm getting there. It helps to hear."

"I think you'll find the Knight women are very good at telling you all that."

"I guess it's good I found me one, then."

"Yeah, it is." She moved onto her toes and kissed him. Without fear, without stress. Just the two of them.

His grip tightened, but the kiss remained gentle. Explorative. Because that's exactly what they had ahead of them.

They'd found each other, and somehow ended years of fear. Of worry. Of dark shadows.

Now, they didn't have to worry anymore. They could get to know each other as something more than friends, find a way to have a life together. With their family.

Happily-ever-after.

* * * * *

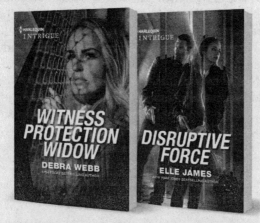

"Two cops broke into your house?" He didn't bother to take out the skepticism. "Did they have a warrant? Did they ID themselves?"

Ashlyn shook her head. "They were wearing uniforms, badges and all the gear that cops have. They used a stun gun on me." She rubbed her fingers along the side of her arm, and the trembling got worse. "They took Cora, but I heard them say they were working for you."

Eli's groan was even louder than the one she made. "And you believed them." The look he gave her was as flat as his tone. He didn't spell out to her that she'd been gullible, but he was certain Ashlyn had already picked up on that.

She squeezed her eyes shut a moment. "I panicked. Wasn't thinking straight. As soon as I could move, I jumped in my car and drove straight here."

The drive wouldn't have taken that long since Ashlyn's house was only about ten miles away. She lived on a small ranch on the other side of Longview Ridge that she'd inherited from her grandparents, and she made a living training and boarding horses.

HIEXP0720

"Did the kidnappers make a ransom demand?" he pressed. "Or did they take anything else from your place?"

"No. They only took Cora. Who brought her here?" Ashlyn asked, her head whipping up. "Was it those cops?"

"Fake cops," Eli automatically corrected. "I didn't see who left her on my porch, but they weren't exactly quiet about it. She was probably out here no more than a minute or two before I went to the door and found her."

He paused, worked through the pieces that she'd just given him and it didn't take him long to come to a conclusion. A bad one. These fake cops hadn't hurt the child, hadn't asked for money or taken anything, but they had let Ashlyn believe they worked for him. There had to be a good reason for that. Well, "good" in their minds, anyway.

"This was some kind of sick game?" she asked.

It was looking that way. A game designed to send her after him.

"They wanted me to kill you?" Ashlyn added a moment later.

Before Eli answered that, he wanted to talk to his brother and get backup so he could take Ashlyn and the baby into Longview Ridge. First to the hospital to confirm they were okay and then to the sheriff's office so he could get an official statement from Ashlyn.

"You really had no part in this?" she pressed.

Eli huffed, not bothering to answer that. He took out his phone to make that call to Kellan, but he stopped when he saw the blur of motion on the other side of Ashlyn's car. He lifted his hand to silence her when Ashlyn started to speak, and he kept looking.

Waiting.

Then, he finally saw it. Or rather he saw them. Two men wearing uniforms, and they had guns aimed right at the house.

Don't miss
Settling an Old Score *by Delores Fossen,*
available August 2020 wherever
Harlequin Intrigue books and ebooks are sold.

Harlequin.com

Love Harlequin romance?

DISCOVER.

Be the first to find out about promotions, news and exclusive content!

 Facebook.com/HarlequinBooks

Twitter.com/HarlequinBooks

Instagram.com/HarlequinBooks

Pinterest.com/HarlequinBooks

ReaderService.com

EXPLORE.

Sign up for the Harlequin e-newsletter and download a free book from any series at **TryHarlequin.com**

CONNECT.

Join our Harlequin community to share your thoughts and connect with other romance readers!
Facebook.com/groups/HarlequinConnection

HARLEQUIN

Heartfelt or suspenseful, inspiring or passionate, Harlequin has your happily-ever-after.

With new books published
every month, you are sure to find the
satisfying escape you know you deserve.